REMEMBER HOW I TOLD YOU I LOVED YOU?

Stories

Gillian Linden

Little
a

Text copyright © 2013 Gillian Linden
All rights reserved.
Printed in the United States of America.
No part of this book may be reproduced, or stored in a retrieval system, or transmitted in any form or by any means, electronic, mechanical, photocopying, recording, or otherwise, without express written permission of the publisher.

Front Cover Design by Chip Kidd
Cover art © Oote Boe Photography

Published by Little A
PO Box 400818
Las Vegas, NV 89140

ISBN-13: 9781477807620
ISBN-10: 1477807624
Library of Congress Control Number: 2013904882

REMEMBER HOW I TOLD YOU I LOVED YOU?

FOR MY MOM

CONTENTS

COMMON ROOMS

Karen meets her in the fall of freshman year. She has another roommate at the time, a scowling brunette named Julie, assigned by the college. That relationship isn't going well. Julie brings home cups of macaroni and ketchup from the dining hall and leaves them on the windowsill in the room. Karen throws away the cups because Julie doesn't, and she keeps finding noodles on the floor. They don't see each other much. Julie has a car and spends a lot of time chauffeuring her friends to the outlet mall, the movies, the sushi restaurant one town away. Every weekend she visits her boyfriend in Vermont.

Karen meets Lizzie, whom she'll think of as her real college roommate, in her English seminar. They're different. Lizzie has glossy hair, she's outgoing, she's from California. When the seminar teacher asks everyone in the class to share something representative, Lizzie says she's addicted to sunlight. She adds that she used to be on track to be a professional figure skater. Karen says she likes open spaces—fields, meadows—and she also likes bread.

Friendship seems unlikely, but they're brought together by two things: both went to Italy recently and discovered limoncello, and both think their seminar teacher is sleeping with a classmate, a girl who has a silver stud in the crease of her nostril. They both admire the stud. Lizzie says it's made her consider getting a nose ring.

Karen and Lizzie have meals together. Lizzie tells Karen about her on-and-off boyfriend, who ended things the day before she left for college. After they graduate, she'll write Karen saying this boyfriend married young and has two kids already. *It kind of wigs me out*, she'll write. And a year after that, at Lizzie's wedding, Karen will have a good conversation with the old boyfriend about a tree next to the wedding site. The tree is surrounded by thick, snaky roots, and the boyfriend will call it enchanted. Karen will feel they've connected.

Now, all Karen knows about him is that he's hurt her friend. "Asshole," she says, and tells the story of her on-and-off boyfriend who went to the prom with a girl who looked like her from behind. She rests her elbows on the dining hall table, which is old and wooden and sticky with jam.

"Everything here is dirty," she says.

"Tell me about it," says Lizzie.

They spend the year together. Karen drinks too much and wakes with bad memories: laughing loudly; gazing into the eyes of someone who, in hindsight, wasn't gazing back; burping. Later she'll read an article about liver disease and wonder if this time has damaged her health; now she's grateful for Lizzie, who holds her up when she slips on the ice walking home and soothes her embarrassment the next day. "No no," she says. "Who cares?" It's not the words—Lizzie's presence makes Karen feel better.

Lizzie has a string of little relationships that year. She dates a few soccer players, a painter, a biology major, a senator in the student council, and four guys on the track team, one of whom almost went to the Olympics. She dumps everyone except the senator. When he stops calling, Lizzie won't leave her room. Karen visits her. She's sitting on her bed, sorting loose change into paper rolls from the bank.

"To keep busy," she says.

She has a classical music station on, the volume too high. There's a violin—it seems to be keening from the center of Karen's brain. Tears have given Lizzie's face a malleable look—pink and soft, as though if you pressed her cheek, the mark would stay. Karen's first impulse is to leave. Then she wants to advise Lizzie to move the coins off the bed. There's already a cloudy spot and a pile of debris on her comforter. She wonders how Lizzie got the rolls for the coins. Did she go to the bank? The tellers there are not friendly. Karen feels a pinch in her throat, a good feeling. She turns down the music and sits on the bed. She's shy about touching people who are upset, but she pats Lizzie's shoulder. "Let me do the nickels," she says.

Soon, Lizzie makes a full recovery. Karen runs into her after a class. Lizzie is eating a banana and wearing new pants.

"What do you think?" she asks.

They're maroon corduroys, comfortable looking and also sleek. Karen thinks, Have Lizzie's legs always been so thin? She says, "I love them."

Lizzie says, "You should get them!"

"I can't. We can't have the same pants."

"Oh, please—why not?"

Karen buys a pair in blue.

Karen has her own moments of vulnerability. At the end of winter she is in a relationship with a guy who wears a suede fedora. When they first meet, she isn't drawn to him. The hat seems like a costume—his personality must be thin. As they spend time together, her perspective shifts. He tells Karen he spends the summer on a fishing boat in Alaska. She pictures him on the dark, sloshy ocean, imagines he has unseen depths. He tells her his father is always at work and his mother has an autoimmune disorder. She's tired all the time. He says that when he lived at home he cooked for his mother. He worries that without him she'll stop eating.

Karen is touched he's so caring. She passes the information on to Lizzie, sitting on the lawn in front of the physics building, sharing a bag of gummy sharks.

"We had the longest talk. He really opened up."

Lizzie sees it differently. She says, "That sounds awful for him. Is he OK?"

Karen considers this. "It is awful." She thinks more and a phrase pops into her head, something a cousin once said about her boyfriend. "He's OK. He possesses silent strength."

"What is *that*?" says Lizzie.

Karen picks up a brown leaf and begins to shred it. "He's resourceful."

Her shirt has drifted up and the hem is bothering her waist. Her back is cool where the air meets her skin. The candy and alcohol and dining hall food ("Loaded with salt," says Lizzie) have left a mark. Karen's clothes are too small. When she sees her family during winter break, her aunt will exclaim, "Finally! You have hips!" Now she pulls down her shirt, tugs her pants, and wonders at how comfortable Lizzie looks, as if the earth underneath her were a pillow. Lizzie examines the marshmallow belly of one of the sharks. "What do you think is in these?"

"I wanted to…" Karen says to the guy with the fedora, that night in her room.

He turns to her, waiting.

"The thing about your mom? It must be scary for you." She's concerned about him and worried about her earlier lack of concern. Was she callous?

4

But there are no hard feelings; he responds warmly to her interest. It was difficult at home, he says, but it's worse being away. So he's considering dropping out of school, despite a scholarship. There are other problems. Someone in his dorm is in a messy relationship. She cries all night.

"Annoying," says Karen.

"No." He puts his elbows on his knees. "Hearing people cry makes me sad."

If this is true, Karen thinks, he really is sensitive.

And he's torn between majoring in psychology and art history. He's interested in both and can't decide.

Karen says he must stay in school—he owes it to himself. She suggests he double major. She tells him not to think about the weeping girl. Some people cry all the time. Karen herself cries a lot, but she's completely fine. The girl is probably completely fine. Anyway, there's nothing he can do about it.

Karen tells Lizzie he's the most authentic person she's ever met. He's handsome when he takes his fedora off, and she even likes the hat. His attachment to it is sweet. When he breaks up with Karen because he's fallen in love with the girl in his dorm, she takes it hard. The night is thicker than it was before, the wind rougher. She starts wearing sunglasses everywhere.

"Come on," Lizzie says when she runs into Karen in her dark glasses, underneath an umbrella, in the rain.

"This has gone on too long," she says. "You barely knew him."

At the end of the year, Karen and Lizzie plan their future together. Lizzie, who claims to have good luck, draws in the room lottery on their behalf.

"I'm telling you," she says, when she's out of the assembly, "sometimes I feel like I have a little rabbit's foot in my pocket." She hands Karen the slip of folded-up white paper. She's drawn second choice.

That fall, they move into a suite on the third floor of a turreted building in the center of campus. Two small bedrooms and a large common area where Lizzie hangs a paper lantern. This is the only year they'll live together. Lizzie has a new seriousness because of a situation at home. She thinks her parents might separate.

"I won't be able to handle it," she says. "How did you deal with it?"

Karen was two when her parents got divorced. She has no memories of them together, no memories of them splitting up. But she wants to help.

"It's hard," she says. "But the fighting is hard too."

Lizzie says, "Sometimes I think my mother *should* leave my dad."

"Really?" Karen's met Lizzie's dad. He's an obstetrician, a bland-looking man with a long torso and a sloping belly, one of those people who seem to be slowly sinking into the earth. He's formal and kind. Last year he called in a prescription for a yeast infection so Karen wouldn't have to make an appointment with student health.

Lizzie looks straight at Karen. "No. Not really. But sometimes I wonder if my father is having an affair."

But who would have sex with him? "You think so?"

"No," she says. "But statistically, it's likely. Seventy-five percent of married men cheat."

"Where did you hear that?"

"I don't remember." Lizzie walks to the window.

It's a warm fall. Karen is lying on the futon with the weak fan on the coffee table directed at her neck.

"Shall we have some limoncello?" says Lizzie.

The minifridge in the common area is given over to the stuff; it was one of the first things they did when they moved in. The thing is, Karen's lost her taste for limoncello. It's too sweet, too syrupy; it's given her too many stomachaches. She hasn't told Lizzie; it's a difficult thing to say.

"Sure," she says. "I'll get the glasses."

Lizzie doesn't mention her parents' marriage again. Sometimes Karen thinks she made the whole thing up. She seems to have had a boring summer. She was a lifeguard at a beach twice a week, perfected a recipe for granola, ran every day. Karen didn't do much either, but inactivity suits her. She likes to read.

They share a bathroom with a suite across the hall. Karen and Lizzie hate the other girls. They're always shouting, they walk heavily up the stairs, they hog the showers. In the morning when Karen goes in to brush her teeth, the mirrors are dripping with condensation.

"This is how you get mold," she tells Lizzie, opening up the window, pushing a snowdrift off the ledge.

Karen's mother grew up in a damp house and passed on a fear of mold. When Karen's older and looking for an apartment, she'll find that every place in her price range has soft gray spots on the grout in the bathroom, in the kitchen behind the sink. Out of necessity, she'll stop caring so much. Now, mold is something she has control over. She thinks she does.

"It's too cold to keep the window open," Lizzie says.

"Just for a few minutes."

At night the girls across the hall bring men into the showers and have sex with them. At first Karen only suspects this is happening, but one evening Lizzie, a little drunk, goes to take out her contacts and sees it: skin pushed against the glass door—someone's thigh, someone's hand. Karen buys flip-flops with platform soles to increase the distance between her feet and the bathroom floor.

"I almost fell trying not to touch the sides of the stall," Lizzie says the morning after her discovery.

A few weeks later, Karen becomes so upset listening to the shower that she begins to cry.

"Not that guy again," Lizzie says.

Earlier in the evening Karen saw the guy with the fedora at her friend's party, on the couch with his new girlfriend. She was holding the hat in her lap, petting its brim as though it were a puppy. Karen used to do the same thing.

"The couch!" Lizzie says.

"Yes, but—"

"You know how it's always kind of damp?"

Karen nods.

Lizzie shivers. "You couldn't pay me to sit on that couch."

It's spring. The trees are covered with blossoms that look like popcorn. Lizzie is doing well romantically. She's dating somebody named Brian, a diver on the diving team. Karen won't know how well she's doing until after they graduate, when Brian becomes her husband. Now he's only a good-looking and talented athlete. Karen doesn't envy the relationship yet. On the weekends they wake up early, put on sneakers, head to the gym. She sometimes meets them afterward for breakfast. Lizzie looks raw. Her hair is wet from the shower and clumps together, leaving bits of scalp visible.

Karen goes with Lizzie to a few of Brian's diving competitions. They wince when he jumps. He shaves his body, and his skin is white and smooth. When he pauses on the edge of the board, he could pass for a wax replica of himself. Karen doesn't tell Lizzie this.

She still thinks about—and sometimes dreams about—the guy with the fedora but time passes and eventually she notices other people. One is in her Introduction to Hinduism class. From far away he's plain, but up close parts of him are beautiful, especially his eyes, which are droopy and pale blue.

Ethan is a philosophy major, and Karen assumes he must be smart. Certainly he is smarter than Karen, smarter than Lizzie, and smarter than Brian. Soon, she'll change her mind. Ethan isn't as smart as any of them, especially not Brian, who is perceptive ("you seem unsettled," he often says to Karen) and excels in his classes. Ethan is not excelling in anything, as far as Karen knows, and he can be imperceptive, especially about Karen and her friends. He calls Willa, whom Karen met through Lizzie, "the mean girl." But Willa is just flaky and shy.

Lizzie, pleased with Brian, wants Karen to be pleased with Ethan. She sees the good in him. Karen tells her his apartment has cockroaches, and a family of pigeons lives outside his window. "Pigeon eggs," she says. Lizzie's scared of pigeons—she ducks when they fly near her—but she won't acknowledge it. She says Brian is thinking of moving off campus, to an apartment with a real kitchen. Karen tells her about the food Ethan makes in his kitchen: boiled hot dogs, spinach prepared with a full stick of butter. Lizzie says it's nice he's cooking. She calls the stick of butter "sort of adorable." Karen relies on her positive outlook. She exposes the worst parts of her relationship, and Lizzie makes her feel better about them.

"I'm not sure I care about him enough," Karen says. "Sometimes I hate him."

"It's impossible not to feel that way when you're spending so much time together." Lizzie frowns. "If you don't want to be with him, that's OK too."

"I don't really hate him. I didn't mean that."

In their junior year, they each have a single on the top floor of the same turreted building. Brian essentially moves in with Lizzie. Over the summer, they have visited each other's families, traveled together to Turkey. "Oh my god, the baklava," Lizzie says.

Karen is still involved with Ethan. He asked her to move into his apartment but she put him off. "I won't get any work done," she said. This has some truth. Recently she's been applying herself. She's taking a literature class on the afterlife in which *she* is excelling and she's stopped drinking except on weekends and some Wednesdays. Ethan thinks her temperance is a drag. "Remember when you used to be fun?" he says.

In the fall, Karen has her first and only fight with Lizzie. It's a cold day in November. She makes a plan to meet her at a health food place. Karen arrives hungry and on time. Lizzie is late. Karen becomes irritated and asks herself whether the lateness is the cause. Ethan says she picks fights about one thing when there's really something else bothering her. When she was annoyed about the buttery spinach, he said, "This can't really upset you."

That time he was wrong—she thought the way he cooked spinach was, in the language of her old seminar teacher, representative— but other times he's been right. Now, about Lizzie, Karen isn't sure. She thinks it's the lateness—what else is there?—but Lizzie's lack of punctuality hasn't bothered her before. Maybe it's that Lizzie is *so often* late. Still, Karen thinks of herself as the kind of person who doesn't get worked up about things like this. When Lizzie finally arrives, Karen won't meet her eyes. She's angry and ashamed of her anger.

"Are you OK?" Lizzie asks.

"I have a headache," Karen says.

"Want a Tylenol?" She reaches for her bag.

"No thanks."

"Are you sure?" she presses.

Karen accepts the Tylenol. She does have a small headache. Now she wants to make amends. "How about you come over some night this week? We can watch TV, have limoncello?"

"Sounds great," says Lizzie. "Except I don't like limoncello anymore. I think because of that cold. All those citrus cough drops." She says Brian and his team are traveling to China in the summer for a competition. "I'm going with him," she says. "I have to get a visa."

But Karen is still thinking about limoncello, which is appetizing again.

Over the summer, while Lizzie is in China, Karen cheats on Ethan with a waiter at the restaurant where she's a hostess. Ethan is at school, working in the rare-books library. Karen is living at her mother's house. The waiter is a little older, and before anything happens Karen spends a long time trying to figure out why he's attractive. He has a square head. His eyes are small. But he rarely smiles, which makes each time he does seem genuine and special. Speaking to him, Karen feels like she's in a class, trying to do well.

A month passes before she goes home with him. His apartment is in an industrial neighborhood with large, stone buildings and scrappy trees. A thin wall, which stops a couple feet short of the ceiling, separates his bedroom from the living room, where his roommate is playing a video game. This is disappointing, as is what happens between them, and on the subway ride to her mother's apartment, Karen mostly feels sorry for herself. By the time she's home she feels guilty too.

She calls in sick to work and doesn't respond to messages from Ethan or the waiter. She does write to Lizzie, though she can't bring herself to confess what she's done. She writes that she's enjoying the restaurant, that she orders tuna tartare off the menu at the end of the night, that the other week a man proposed to his girlfriend in the back garden. Lizzie replies immediately. She burned her tongue on soup dumpling, she's reading essays about California, she's homesick.

Homesick is how Karen feels, though she doesn't miss home, more like an earlier version of herself, a person who, in her memory, is hardworking, straightforward, pure.

She stays in bed. Her mother brings pretzels and ginger ale as though she really is sick. She puts a hand on Karen's forehead. "You don't have a temperature."

"I think I ate something." Karen rolls away. "I don't want to work at the restaurant anymore."

"I can't hear you."

"I'm going to quit."

"You've had it?"

Karen's mother never wanted her to work at a restaurant. She wanted her to get an internship at a magazine, or a law firm, or a not for profit. She considers Karen's quitting a victory, though there are only a few weeks of summer left, not enough time to find something else.

Karen is sure that she'll feel guilty about the waiter forever but that turns out not to happen. Soon she decides it's Ethan's fault. He's withdrawn, temperamental, a bad cook. Still, it takes until the middle of their fourth year of college for Karen to break up with him.

One night, in the middle of senior year, Karen is studying at Ethan's apartment. She sits on his bed with a pillow behind her and another on top of her feet to keep them warm. Ethan is at his desk, working on his computer, on a chart, which looks like a big, bright cobweb. It's raining outside. He lives on the top floor and several times Karen hears the wind whistle around the walls and thinks it's the teakettle. Her book is about a factory town in northern England. The life of the factory worker is hard, much harder than hers. Still, she relates to certain conditions—the coldness of the supervisors, the terrible weather. The town she lives in has bad weather too, and there's plenty of coldness in her life.

"I don't think we should continue this," she says.

"Continue what?"

"This." Karen makes a circular movement with her hand in the space between them, like she's stirring up a tiny storm.

She explains: he won't walk her back to her dorm at night, even though the walk is through a bad neighborhood; when he lightly sprained his ankle, he refused to go anywhere for a week, and she had to do all his errands; the romance between them has evaporated—they haven't had sex in six weeks. The only thing she doesn't mention is the way he made her cheat on him with the waiter.

Three days after this conversation, Ethan starts seeing someone from the rare-books library, a woman whose hair is very similar to Karen's. She remembers her high school boyfriend and the girl who looked like her from behind. Why does this keep happening? She accrues a two-hundred-dollar cell-phone bill calling her friends from home and tracks Ethan through his instant-message statuses. Twice when she knows he's there, she goes to his apartment. The first time, he lets her in. She sits on the floor in his living room. She says, "I feel awful."

"Why don't you get up, anyway." Ethan pats the spot next to him. "Come on the couch."

"Why are you doing this?"

"I'm sorry about…you know…" He opens his hand, like he's presenting her to an audience, to herself. He's looking at her closely. She thinks, Did he always look at me with such focus? He's almost dignified, sitting with his legs crossed. He has long fingers. His body is elegant, like a tree. "I'm worried about you," he says. "But let's please be clear: this was your decision."

The second time she goes over, he won't open the door. "I'm not letting you in," he says. "I don't think it's a good idea."

Lizzie is sympathetic, but she spends so much time with Brian she's not always available to talk.

They're closer than ever, Lizzie and Brian. Something has happened to their faces: they resemble each other around the mouth and in the shape of their eyes. Charlotte, Karen's friend from home, to whom she describes it, says it's weird, but Karen thinks it's a sign of how they're adapting to each other. Lizzie *is* lucky, Karen thinks. She's right about that rabbit's foot.

They don't see each other often in the spring of senior year. Lizzie is an economics major and she's being recruited by credit-card companies and investment banks. She spends weekends traveling around the country for interviews. Once, she flies to London to meet with some executives. The rest of her time is taken up with Brian. Karen cultivates new friendships: with a photographer who takes pictures of his feet; with a house of people who are all on a macrobiotic diet; with Lizzie's friend Willa, who drops by every once in a while to watch a few episodes of *Law & Order*.

Lizzie's parents arrive together for graduation weekend. Her mother is wearing a blue skirt and carrying a large camera. She takes a picture of Karen before she says hello. Lizzie's father shakes Karen's hand and tells her congratulations.

Karen's parents are there too, and her mother's new boyfriend. Over dinner the night before the ceremony, they talk about her life. She was slender for a baby, had nice smelling skin. She had bronchitis and eczema. She talked early, walked late, and never crawled.

"I did see you shuffle a couple of times," her father says.

"You were darling," her mother says.

Her mother's boyfriend asks what her plans are.

Lizzie stops by while she's packing. She has her hair in two braids, and Karen is surprised by how young she looks. They're both emotional when they say good-bye. The color of Lizzie's skin seems to become unblended—patches of red and cream, as though each pigment were joining up with its kind. Karen thinks of her on her bed with the coins.

"You'll have to visit me," Lizzie says.

"I will."

"I told Brian. The futon is reserved for you." She pulls at Karen's hand.

"I can't wait to test it out." Karen is thinking the chances of her spending a night on the futon are slim—Lizzie's moving across the country. She begins to cry. She may never see Lizzie again.

Eventually, Karen goes to Lizzie's wedding, and Lizzie goes to Karen's, and in between there are other weddings they both attend. Karen spends the night on Lizzie's futon and then her foldout couch and then a bed in her guest room. The room has wooden floors painted white and reminds Karen of the suite they shared in college. Lizzie's old desk is in it, pushed up against the window.

But there are people Karen doesn't see much of after she graduates. She's in touch with Ethan for a bit and then, somehow, she's not anymore. She doesn't see any of the people from the macrobiotic household, though she wishes she did. She never sees the guy with the fedora, but Willa does. He's recently returned from Germany, and Willa says he's smaller. Karen asks her to explain, but she can't; he just seemed smaller in every way. "Even his head," she says. People shrink—it happens all the time with the elderly—but Karen thinks it's a shame he's starting to shrink so young. She wonders if his hat still fits. She's sorry for him, and this makes her feel good.

REMEMBER HOW I TOLD YOU I LOVED YOU

Daphne spent the summer doing nothing—lying around Dennis's bedroom in his parents' apartment. They'd been together since June. She'd graduated and had a job lined up for late October in the development office of a college. Dennis was on summer vacation. They'd taken picnics to the riverbank, the botanical gardens, and a small park near Daphne's parents' place, where they tried to carve their initials into a tree. It was hard. The knife they brought, a stainless-steel cleaver, couldn't get the job done, and they gave up after the first *D*. Daphne assumed it stood for her name until the walk back, when she realized it might stand for Dennis.

"Whose name were you working on?" she asked. His arm was over her shoulder and her arm was around his waist, bony and warm. "Is the *D* for Daphne or Dennis?"

"It can be for both of us."

They were silent for a block, then Daphne said, "What were you thinking when we started?"

Dennis looked up. A blimp was passing overhead. "No idea. Let's say your name."

It was late August. Daphne had freckles and Dennis was golden and glowing, as if he'd taken in so much light he could give some of it back. He had to return to school.

"You could come," he said after he'd thrown his last bag into the car.

"Now?" Daphne peered into the backseat—crumbs and papers and a pillow in a blue case. "I don't have my things."

"Not now. Meet me."

"But I'm starting work. I need the money."

"Get a job there." Dennis sat on the hood. "You could find a job anywhere."

Daphne was silent.

"Why not?" he said.

The bus ride was five hours with a break at a convenience store on the side of the highway. There was a brown field behind the store where Daphne ate a banana, shifting her weight from one leg to the other. Her seatmate was nearby, stretching. She was thin, older than Daphne; she had white in her hair. Unfolded to her full height, she was taller than most of the male passengers. "They really pack us in," she said.

"It's like the subway," said Daphne.

"Oh, I don't take the subway," the woman said. "I can't be underground."

Back on the bus, Daphne tried several positions but couldn't get comfortable. She put her head against the window, which sent vibrations through her skull. She leaned back and propped her knees on the seat in front of her, but her thigh went numb. She put her seat back a couple of inches, and the man sitting behind her kicked it. She kept her seat where it was. Let him kick.

She looked out the window. There was an empty school bus in the next lane. She had to call the development office, tell them she couldn't take the job. And she had to send out resumes. She'd do that as soon as she got to Dennis's. Maybe there'd be something at his school. Going over this was soothing, like making the bed. The woman next to Daphne fell asleep, her head dropping closer and closer to Daphne's shoulder. It really was like the subway.

The road narrowed. The woods on the side of the highway were thick; they looked wild. Daphne wondered if anyone lived in there. As a child she'd read a few books about boys living in hollowed-out trees.

It wouldn't take long to find something. She was very employable—everyone said so. She'd been a popular babysitter growing up, and she'd answered the phone at the dean's office during college. She was responsible and competent—everyone said that too. "You don't know what a blessing it is," one mother declared, "having you nearby." It was as though Daphne were gifted. Of course she wasn't, not for that reason. Anyone could be competent. It was a matter of showing up on time and staying a little late, and, if anything went wrong—if a cup of tea spilled on some files, if a baby rolled off the bed—not telling anyone about it.

The bus turned and Daphne's seatmate woke up. "Goodness, I'm sorry." She lifted her head. There were soft, shallow wrinkles all over her face.

"It's completely OK," Daphne said. "This actually happens to me all the time."

The woman remained silent for a moment, looking at Daphne. "How long was I out?"

"Not so long."

The terminal was deserted when they arrived.

"You seem like a very nice young woman," Daphne's seatmate said when they said good-bye.

Dennis was outside, waiting in his car. All the junk was still in the back, but the front was clear. He lifted her hand and kissed her palm, looking serious; then he laughed.

She said, "Have you been drinking?"

"No—just waiting. You're late."

"It felt long."

"Half an hour. Come on. Let's get home."

Dennis lived in a gray wooden house with a screened-in porch and a few old trees in front. He shared the house with a guy named Ed and Ed's cat, Pepper. Ed was taller than Dennis. He had short, orderly hair, like the green of a golf course. His father had recently left his mother for a physical therapist.

"It is messing with Ed's head," Dennis said. "Big time."

But Ed never mentioned it, and his head seemed, if not spectacularly healthy, fine. He spent a lot of time studying and watching political talk shows on cable, which he said relaxed him. "The tone is very consistent," he said. "I know some people see that as a flaw."

He did have a collection of pharmaceuticals in the upstairs bathroom. Daphne discovered it when she went looking for Pepper, who was curled in the sink, letting the faucet drip down her fur. She picked the cat up and opened the medicine cabinet. There were two rows of orange pill bottles on the bottom shelf, most of them with names Daphne didn't recognize. Dennis said they were for pain. "Ed had some shoulder injury a few years ago."

"I thought they might have to do with the family situation," said Daphne. "Mood stabilizers, you know."

"I don't think so. That's what Pepper's for."

Pepper was Ed's family cat and usually lived with his parents. Now she slept in his bed at night and stalked the house during the day, pawing at the place where the wall met the floor.

"She catches insects," Ed said, scratching Pepper's neck.

"I didn't know you had insects," Daphne said. "I haven't seen any."

"I would hope not. Right, Pepper? I would certainly hope Daphne hasn't seen any insects."

They were at a Tex-Mex restaurant, a place near the grocery store where Dennis worked some afternoons. A quesadilla was between them. Pale and dry, it reminded Daphne of a manila folder.

The job search was stalled. She'd distributed resumes, sent them to departments in Dennis's school and a couple not-for-profits— one concerned with women in science, the other wetlands. She'd hand-delivered them to coffee shops and a clothing store. It had been a week.

"Give it more time," said Dennis. He paused, as if considering his next words. Daphne thought of his struggle carving the *D* into the tree. "Come on," he said. "Don't go back."

"It's not that I don't want to stay," said Daphne.

"I love having you here." He frowned. "I love you."

Dennis was curious. He was usually reserved, but then there were these outbursts. It was quiet in the restaurant; it was lunch-time. Daphne put down her fork and peeled off a sliver of tortilla. Dennis tugged her sleeve. She glanced at him and was surprised by how nice he looked: thin and small and neat.

"I love you too," she said.

He leaned over the table and kissed her, but when he moved away one of her hairs snagged on the corner of his glasses and pulled her scalp, making her flinch.

"What's wrong?" he said.

"Nothing." Daphne touched the sore spot.

"What?"

She thought of the kicking man on the bus. "Really nothing." She smiled. "I was remembering something."

Dennis looked at the quesadilla as if he didn't trust it. He cut a small bite. "You're inscrutable," he said.

"You think so?" said Daphne. "I think you are."

"No you. Very mysterious."

Daphne had a message from Isabel, "calling to say hi." She returned it from Dennis's bed while he was at class.

"Dennis said he loved me."

"You hadn't said that yet?"

"No."

"Well, what did you say?" Isabel had been with the same guy for years. She liked to think about other people's relationships.

"That I loved him."

"Do you?"

"I don't know."

"You didn't have to say it back."

"That's so *awkward*." Daphne had a bowl of muesli on her stomach. She brushed oats off her shirt. "I'm a little obsessed with Dennis. I might love him."

"Would you be upset if he died?"

"Obviously."

"I mean really upset."

"I can't imagine it."

"But would you give up something for him?"

"Like money?"

"You don't have any money. A kidney or something."

Daphne felt around her midsection. "Where are your kidneys?"

"I think on your back. My father had the worst backache when he had a kidney infection."

Daphne touched the soft skin on her back. She had a weak feeling in her stomach imagining Isabel's father's infected kidneys.

She wiggled her legs. "I think I'd give him a kidney. Or I don't know. I'd have to find out more about it. Would you give Sean a kidney?"

"Of *course.*"

Daphne set her bowl of muesli on the floor. "I have to go. I have a mountain of cleaning."

"I bet you do."

Pepper was the first member of the household to eat each day. Dennis and Ed didn't have breakfast, and Daphne fed Pepper before she made herself anything. It was her contribution while she looked for work. When she had something, she'd pay rent. For now, she did small chores—sweeping the porch, some laundry, feeding Pepper. They hadn't asked her to do this. Ed had even asked her not to—he said it made him feel funny. Daphne said not doing anything made *her* feel funny. Dennis said it wasn't a big deal, that nobody needed to feel funny one way or the other.

Pepper's food was underneath the sink. When Daphne opened the lid the cat trotted into the kitchen and pushed herself into Daphne's shins, and, when Daphne stooped to put the dish on the floor, Pepper lifted onto her hind legs to meet it.

"Hey," Daphne said. "It's not like you're starving."

But soon she wondered if Pepper might be starving—you couldn't pat her without feeling bones—and began giving her extra pellets.

Dennis made dinner almost every night. Watching him whisk a dressing or mince garlic made Daphne proud. Sometimes she'd put a hand on his back, underneath his shirt. Sometimes she'd just watch him. It was like that song "Hungry Eyes." She didn't really understand it until she saw Dennis cook. And it turned out Daphne was not such a mystery because Dennis picked up on something in the way she looked at him. He'd say, "Stop *looking* at me," and if she didn't stop, he'd send her to the other room to watch TV with Ed. Ed was right: the tone of his shows was very consistent.

"How are the interviews coming?"

Daphne had told her mother that the job market was promising and now she did have an interview—she'd gotten the voicemail that morning. In fact, it hadn't taken long for something to turn up—just a couple weeks.

"I have one next week at a clinic."

"Oh?"

"The psych clinic at school. They need a receptionist."

"That sounds fine."

"I think they'll pay decently. Plus the benefits."

"How are you liking it there?"

It was cold, even though it was only September, and Daphne's social life was thin. Ed and Dennis were always in class or at work and she still didn't know anyone else. On the other hand, Dennis's grocery store sold a nut mix, which Daphne would eat in the afternoons, sitting in a jacket on the porch, reading magazines. And Dennis looked cozy in sweaters. Sometimes Daphne considered moments in her day from the outside and liked the idea of them, even though she hadn't enjoyed being in them at all.

"It's nice," she said. "The air smells good." Even in the house there was a woodsy smell.

"I have a question," said her mother. "If I send you an e-mail and I BCC three other people, can they see all the addresses?"

"Only mine." Daphne wandered with the phone to the front door to look for Dennis.

"That's what I thought. So talk to you soon? Be sure to wear a hat."

Daphne put on a hat and walked to the end of the driveway. Each day Dennis came home a few minutes later than the day before.

Their room was next to the kitchen. It had a mattress on the floor and poli-sci books against the wall. The window looked into the back, where there was a metal fence grown over with vines, and on the other side, a house similar to Dennis's but blue. Dennis had hitched yellow fabric to a curtain rod, but it slipped off at least once a day. Daphne thought about the moment when the cloth dropped. Was it because of a breeze? Or gravity? Was it like her seatmate's head on the bus, gradually lowering the whole time? When Dennis noticed it he'd loop it back over the rod, but he never did anything to make it more secure.

"Pin it," Daphne said.

"I've been meaning to get real curtains."

So Daphne fixed it, folding the edge of the rectangle over the curtain rod and pinning it at the corners. It looked worse. It seemed more crooked, even though it had never been straight. She *had* to spend less time in Dennis's bedroom. Her interview was in a few days and soon she'd have a reason to be out of the house for hours on end.

Daphne and Dennis had grown up near each other and dated for a month when they were sixteen. Once, when they were underneath the quilt in his television room, Dennis's mother came in.

"Louise? Is that Louise?"

"No," said Daphne. "It's Daphne."

But actually Daphne got along with Dennis's mother. His father was the problem. During dinner one night the past summer he'd said, "Daphne is awfully good at ingratiating herself." It was so out of place—like seeing a raccoon in daylight—it took them all a moment to understand. Finally Dennis said, "Dad," and his mother said, "God, Paul."

"What?" said Paul. "I'm saying she's a good guest."

Daphne didn't say anything. She tried to laugh, but she couldn't open her lips, like her whole face—her skin and everything—was stuck. She felt as though she'd been hit.

Daphne's father asked, "What do you do there all day?"

"Well"—Daphne shifted the phone to her other ear—"a lot of reading. I've been on some runs." She had planned to jog to Dennis's grocery store earlier, but she gave up in the driveway because it was cold.

But her father approved of jogging. He said a daily twenty-minute jog with no breaks for walking was a key to longevity. The other keys were water and sleep, some fish every week, deep breathing, and vitamins D, B, and C. There were so many keys, Daphne's mother said, that they were not keys at all.

"A key is a trick," she said. "It's *the* thing that makes something else happen."

"Not true," said Daphne's father. "Not always. You can have a door with multiple locks."

Now he said, "Really—are you jogging?"

"Well, it's nicer here than at home. The air smells good."

"That's terrific."

After she hung up, Daphne put on sneakers and a hat and went for a walk around the block. The air smelled like something burning. A few houses down a man was raking the lawn, pausing to put certain leaves in his pocket. So Daphne wasn't the only one with time on her hands. She wondered if Pepper would walk with her— it'd be nice to have company. But Pepper was under the weather. She'd thrown up a few times. Daphne had been meaning to tell Ed.

One afternoon, while Daphne was in bed, a girl came into the house calling Dennis's name.

Daphne walked out. "He's in class," she said.

"Oh hi." The girl said her name was Natalie. "I didn't think he had class now."

"No," said Ed, who was passing the kitchen and stepped in. "He doesn't. He's at the market. Hi, Nat."

Natalie was a nice name—it was the name of one of Daphne's friends growing up, a tall red-haired girl. This Natalie was around the same height as Daphne and had dark hair. She wore a skirt, thick tights. She had thin arms but heavy legs. She probably over-exercises, Daphne thought. Natalie's eyes were deep set. They made her look sophisticated, like she'd seen things. She had brought in chilly air.

"Well." She looked to either side of the kitchen.

"Can I help you with something?" said Daphne. She glanced at Ed. "Can we?"

Natalie looked at Ed. "I think you guys have my juicer. From last year."

"We should, but I haven't seen it. Dennis put it somewhere." Ed began to move around, opening and closing cabinets. He rummaged underneath the sink.

Daphne felt like a guest. This was Ed's kitchen and Dennis's kitchen. Natalie had known this kitchen longer than she had. Daphne was embarrassed, like she'd been caught faking something, but she hadn't been. She belonged there as much—almost as much—as the rest of them. She'd been invited in. There was Pepper, asleep in a bit of sunlight in the corner. Daphne was taking care of Pepper, basically keeping Pepper alive. She joined Ed's search, opening things up, beginning, foolishly, with the cutlery drawer.

Natalie was lingering at the table, flipping through the mail. Her hands were red and calloused. Daphne remembered the pantry around the corner.

"Is this it?" She brought out an old juicer. The plastic had turned dark around the edges.

"That's it." Natalie gathered it into her arms. "Thanks." She turned to Ed. "Thank you." She kissed his cheek.

"Nice to see you around here," Ed said.

Daphne wanted to move Natalie away from him. "I'll tell Dennis you dropped by," she said.

And when Dennis returned, Daphne did tell him that.

He sat on a kitchen chair, handing her a bag of nut mix. "Too bad I missed her."

Daphne picked out an almond. "She seemed nice." Though Natalie hadn't seemed that nice. "We gave her the juicer."

"She's been a good friend." Dennis laughed to himself and said that everyone thought he and Natalie were together.

"Everyone who?" said Daphne.

"Everyone around here." He gestured to the empty kitchen. He said that when Daphne had arrived, people were very confused.

"Which people?" Daphne had barely met anyone. Just Ed and now Natalie and one other guy, Tim or Tom, who'd stopped by to borrow their electric screwdriver.

"Ed, for example," Dennis said. "That's why he was so weird around you at first."

Had Ed been weird around her? She said, "Ed thought so?" Something else occurred to her. "Wouldn't he know? Were you with Natalie?"

"No." Dennis stood and took off his coat. He folded his scarf and put it on the table. He was always careful with his clothes. "Well, almost once, but we're too similar. It'd be like dating myself."

Dennis was a deep sleeper, and even Ed fell asleep at a certain point. In the early morning Daphne stopped hearing his footsteps through the ceiling. But Daphne couldn't sleep, which happened once in a while. One night, when she could still hear Ed's footsteps above them, she knocked on his door.

"Do you have sleeping pills?" she asked.

"Do I have sleeping pills." Ed led Daphne to his medicine cabinet and pulled out a couple of bottles. "I used to have trouble sleeping. Plenty of trouble."

There was a minty smell. "You don't anymore?"

"Not really. Or it's more like, I do but I don't care."

Daphne saw her face in the mirror, a line running down her cheek from the pillow. She was wearing her pajama top and a pair of Dennis's boxers. She looked at her legs, the hair on her knees. What had Ed said? He didn't mind not sleeping? She thought of her dad. "I'm kind of crazy about sleep," she said, and fled downstairs with the pills.

Dennis was behind Daphne in school because he'd gotten sick. He'd contracted hepatitis and had taken a year to convalesce. During that time, he'd dated a model. She was in a denim ad that was on taxicabs all over the city. Dennis said he'd never been that into her, but he talked about her often, her and her model friends.

"Those girls are so thin," he said one night, glancing at a magazine Daphne was flipping through. "You know the camera adds weight."

They were on the porch, drinking hot cider with whiskey. Daphne was sitting on Dennis's lap, his hand on her leg. She stood and moved to a chair next to Ed.

Ed looked at the page. It was a perfume ad, a woman in a filmy white dress. "How much thinner could they be?" He thought the whole thing about models, about good-looking people generally, was pretty silly. He'd said so to Daphne one afternoon when Dennis was at work. "Looks are important," he'd said. "But not *that* important."

"Exactly," said Daphne.

"Well, you should see their arms," Dennis said. "I don't know how they get their skin to stick to their bones."

"What do you mean?" It seemed to Daphne that the thinner somebody was, the more tightly the skin would stick.

"No muscle, no fat." He guessed that models must use some sort of lotion—a special kind that tightened everything.

"Gross," said Daphne. She thought of Pepper. "Ed," she said. "Pepper's been...not feeling well. She's thrown up a couple of times."

"You're only giving her half a cup?"

Daphne looked at him.

"Food? Half a cup?"

"Yes." She'd been giving Pepper a full cup, sometimes a cup and a handful. The cat was so skinny.

"She has a sensitive stomach."

"I give her half a cup. Whatever the scoop in the bag is."

"She could have a virus." Ed stood up and went into the house to look for Pepper.

Daphne's tights were squeezing her stomach. It seemed like it would be for nothing. The head of the psych clinic was out. He was in a grocery-cart race around the town.

"I can't believe he scheduled the interview for now," said the student assistant. "He's had this day on his calendar for months. Don't tell anyone. It's totally illegal."

"Where do they go?" Daphne asked.

"Mostly residential neighborhoods. They steer clear of downtown, avoid the cars."

The office smelled like marinara sauce. There was a half-eaten meatball grinder falling open on a piece of foil on the assistant's desk. He licked his fingers and picked up Daphne's resume. "Do you want me to give him this?"

"That's just an extra," said Daphne. "Maybe better not. Where do they get the carts?"

"They steal them."

Daphne looked behind the assistant into an empty office. There was a black leather chair and a photo of a pink stucco house.

"Listen," said the assistant. "I feel bad that you came all the way out. But I have a sense for these things? Looking at you—" He seemed to take in her clothes—a cardigan, a button-down—which she'd bought for the other job. She'd picked up the phone to call them a couple of times but hadn't gone through with it. It was prudent to wait until something else was lined up.

"You'll get the job if you want it," he said. "Also, between us, the hiring process is not very rigorous."

"When should I come back?" said Daphne. "Or I could call tomorrow? When he's in?"

"That would be ideal."

Daphne lay with her head on Dennis's stomach, which was concave, as though someone's head had made a permanent depression in it. Louise's head, Daphne thought. No, she thought, Natalie's.

She didn't feel much about this. It was as though she was considering someone else's boyfriend, someone else's life.

"Remember how I told you I loved you?" Dennis said. He was winding a section of Daphne's hair around his finger. They were in his bedroom. The curtain was on the ground. Daphne put Natalie out of her mind. She thought about the places they'd gone over the summer, Dennis's warmed-up skin. "I remember," she said.

Dennis dropped the hair and sat up. He looked down at her, directly into her eyes. "I'm not sure if I love you."

It was like that night with his parents, his father insulting her across the roast chicken, except this time she wasn't trying to laugh. She rubbed her forehead.

"Don't cry." Dennis brushed her head with his hand.

"I'm not." She wanted to say she didn't love him either, that she'd only said she did out of consideration for his feelings.

She sat up. Dennis could find his own goddamn kidney. She'd save hers for people she really cared about, for people who cared about her. Please, she'd save them for herself.

Daphne's oldest friend called her.

"I need a roommate," she said. "Are you still out of town?"

"Yes."

"Really," Cynthia said. "Still?"

How long had it been? Just under a month. "The air here smells good."

"What?"

"The air." But it had been so cold recently the air didn't smell like much.

"Well, are you coming back?"

"I think so."

"Decide soon. I have to find someone in a week."

Cynthia had started working for a group that provided legal services for victims of domestic violence. "We just found out there's a brothel two floors beneath our office," she said. "Can you believe that?"

"No." Pepper came into Daphne's lap, straight from outside. She was back to feeding Pepper the right amount and the cat seemed to like her better for it. She'd stopped vomiting. Daphne put her face into Pepper's body, her cool, feathery fur. "Are you still liking the job, though?"

"It's tough. But I do like it. I love it."

"I can't sleep," Daphne said the next night.

Ed went to the bathroom and Daphne waited, sitting on his bed, which, unlike Dennis's, had a frame and was lifted a couple feet off the floor. Ed came back and sat next to her. He put his hand on the ridge of her shoulder and pressed with his fingers, one by one, like he was playing a piano. Daphne felt little bursts of pain—good pain—around her neck. She faced him. Ed was thinner than Dennis. He was like Pepper—you could see his ribs. He was light on top of her and had patches of hair on his chest.

He woke her up while it was still dark. "You should go," he said.

When Daphne came in Dennis lifted his head. "Where were you?"

"Couldn't sleep."

He rolled over, hugging the pillow. Daphne went to the closet and shook out her blue duffel bag. When Dennis woke again, she asked him to take her to the bus.

On the ride home she called the development office of the college and confirmed her start date. It was lucky she hadn't passed up that job. Well, it had nothing to do with luck. It was not acting too quickly, behaving responsibly. It was a sort of life competence, Daphne's gift.

They met at a bar in December. He was home for winter break, and she was living with Cynthia. He had almost completely shaved his hair. It was just a shadow over his skull and it reminded Daphne of the dry field behind the convenience store on the ride to his town.

"You don't like it?" He put his hand behind his ear, where there was a scab.

"I was used to how it was before."

"Come on. You like it."

"Sure, I like it." Daphne smiled. She didn't want to look at it.

They ordered two veggie burgers, but the waiter only brought one so Dennis cut it in half.

"Hey." He put the knife down and looked at Daphne. "I'm sorry about everything."

"Oh, me too," she said.

"All that stuff with Natalie."

Daphne's Natalie, her childhood friend, had executed perfect back dives. Fluid, fearless jumps off the diving board. Once, she'd hit the bottom of the pool and injured her nose. Daphne tried to bring up an image of Dennis's Natalie—the thick legs, the sophisticated eyes. The thing was she didn't seem like a Natalie. She seemed more like a June or a Grace.

"Do you think her name suits her?" Daphne asked. "Don't you think June would be better?"

"I don't know about that." Dennis took a bite of the burger and shifted it into one cheek so he could keep talking. "But she felt terrible about everything. She was *all* worked up."

"What everything?"

"You know."

"Yes." Daphne was slightly surprised and then not surprised at all. She was a little angry.

"Anyway," Dennis said. "Sorry." He tapped the top of her hand. "Really."

Daphne took a sip of water. She wanted to tell Dennis she'd slept with Ed, but he might not believe her now. If he did, Ed might not like it. It would complicate their living situation. Ed had written her an e-mail. *I wish you hadn't gone. Pepper misses you. So do I.*

Once, walking to work, she'd thought she'd seen Ed ahead of her on the street. She'd jogged half the block. The man, thank goodness, had turned to throw something away before she caught him. Of course it wasn't Ed, just somebody tall with dark hair.

"It's fine," Daphne said. "I'm sorry too."

Dennis reached over and tucked Daphne's hair behind her ear. "You don't have anything to be sorry for."

When Daphne got home that night, Avery, Cynthia's cat, was hiding under the couch. Avery had been found on the street when she was about a year old. She was frightened of strangers, the rain, and being alone. She was slim and soft, like Pepper. And Daphne fed her too, because Cynthia worked long hours. She never gave her more than half a cup.

She crouched down. "Avery," she said. "Don't you want supper?" The cat looked at Daphne with big golden eyes.

HAM AND CRACKERS

The nurse, a man named Andy, greets her at the door and says Bette is asleep.

"You're late," he says. "She was expecting you two hours ago."

"The bakery switched my shift," Karen says. "I told her last week."

"Did you? She must've forgotten. She's been off all day. She ate lunch at ten thirty."

"That's more like breakfast."

"Right. I said to her—I said, 'How are you hungry? Didn't you just have breakfast?' She said she got up early this morning."

This is the longest exchange Karen has had with Andy. They don't always overlap, and when she first started visiting Bette he didn't speak to her at all. But now he looks embarrassed and turns to pat the envelopes on the table into a pile, brush dust into his palm. He's wearing a pair of green scrubs and a thin T-shirt that reveals the delicate cut of his shoulder blades. Andy is tall and lean, good-looking in a worn way. His hair is gray.

"Well," Karen says.

"I don't know when she'll wake up." Andy turns back around. "You can go home if you want."

"I'll wait for a bit, in case."

"Suit yourself. There's ham in the kitchen if you're hungry."

He walks toward the back of the apartment. Karen takes off her coat and goes into the living room. She's brought a book—a novel about a man, Greg, who keeps getting let go from jobs, each one worse than the last—but she doesn't want to read it. On the coffee table is a stack of interior design magazines with covers like glass. Karen chooses one and settles into the couch.

Bette is clearly sick. Pill bottles are on the kitchen counter and card games ended early due to fatigue. A few weeks ago her lower left leg puffed up to the size of a small tree trunk. And there's Andy, the nurse. When Karen was a child, the father of one of her classmates had cancer and a nurse started coming to their place. The father was old; he was on his third marriage. His nurse had a baby whom she sometimes brought along, setting him up in the corner of the living room in an electric swing.

Bette may have cancer, maybe some other stuff too, but she never talks about it and Karen doesn't ask. Karen tries to know as little about it as possible, although sometimes it can't be avoided. Last August, when she was helping Bette unpack from a weekend trip, she came across gauze pads.

It was hot. A vase of wildflowers on the dresser was giving off a sharp smell. Bette's suitcase had hidden compartments so that when Karen thought she'd finished, Bette would tell her to lower a panel and unbuckle a strap and a handful of slips or necklaces or a few pairs of underwear would fall out. The whole thing was too intimate, already more than Karen had signed on for. And now these pads, four spongy stacks in a Ziploc bag.

"I don't know what to do with this," Karen said, holding up the bag.

"Here." Bette stretched out her hand. She was supervising from a seat next to the dresser. She fit so perfectly into the contours of the chair that her body disappeared, as if she were just clothing laid out for the next day.

Karen closes the magazine and thinks about reading her book. Greg has just taken a position as a dog walker for an aggressive boxer. The boxer's owners are afraid of the dog. The neighbors are afraid of the dog. Even the vet is afraid of the dog. The only person not afraid of the dog is Greg. Karen senses that things are going to turn around for him.

She scans the living room, looking for her bag, but it must be in the hall. She doesn't want to get up to find it; instead, she lies down. She takes off her shoes and stretches out, puts a cushion underneath her head.

The living room is the prettiest room in the apartment. It has wide plank wooden floors, ancient-looking windows paned with thick glass, an armchair in the corner with a daisy pattern on it. The room is sparsely furnished and feels spacious, but, unlike Karen's idea of spacious places, it's always warm, even now, in winter. Karen returns to the magazine, flipping to a spread of photos of an actor's private island. There are pastel-colored bungalows, infinity pools, and topiary in shapes that recall the actor's movies—a gladiator's helmet, a bowling ball, a puppy with pointy ears.

Karen met Bette through Ethan a couple months before they broke up. They were going to spend the weekend with his parents in Massachusetts.

"Oh, and this old friend of my dad's will be there," Ethan said. "You'll like her—she's a character."

Karen doubted she would like her. When people were called characters it meant that they had a bad personality, which was tolerated because they were wealthy or famous or had lived a long time. And Bette *was* rich, Ethan said. And old.

"How does your dad know her?"

"He knew her husband," Ethan said. "Jerry. He died a few years ago. She's alone now, although she has a child I think, or children. Maybe stepchildren."

Karen didn't mind Bette at first. She liked Bette's emphatic handshake, her clipped accent. When they arrived Bette was wearing a long sweater, a wool skirt, clogs. I'll dress like that someday, Karen thought.

That night, Bette asked Karen to take her to her room. She needed a hand making it up the stairs.

"Will you help me?" she said.

"Sure." Karen said. "Of course."

Bette gathered her things, folding her glasses and putting a book underneath her arm. She was like a forest creature, a squirrel or chipmunk. Karen said, "I can carry something."

Ethan's mother walked in and, seeing the preparations, offered Bette her arm.

"No," Bette said. "The girl said she'd take me."

Karen switches magazines, pulling one from the bottom of the stack. It's from decades ago and not as shiny. The pages are brittle, the colors washed out. This is how Karen thinks of her parents' youth, a softer, duller time.

The girl. Karen hasn't forgiven Bette for that. As if Karen were just a tiny star in Bette's universe. But this wasn't true. Karen was at the heart of the story—at the beginning of her life, everything in front of her—and Bette was peripheral, just a lady with an interesting accent and good clothes, just some tertiary *character* Karen happened to cross paths with.

A year after they split up, Karen and Ethan became friendly again, and when she told him she needed to make more money, he suggested Bette.

"She's mostly looking for a companion," he said. "She already has some sort of medical help. Well, you met her. She doesn't like to be alone. The work would be light, and I'm sure she'd pay well."

Karen said she'd think about it, planning not to follow up. Being paid to just spend time with someone seemed shifty. But she reconsidered. If Bette wanted to hand out money, why shouldn't it be to Karen?

And Ethan was right—the work has been light. They play gin, or Karen reads out loud from the newspaper, or Bette dictates e-mails. *How is Anthony? How is Fofie? Hope to be at camp almost all summer.* Most often, Karen fixes sliced pears or crackers and cheese and they sit in the television room and watch Oprah.

Karen closes her eyes. She should go home. She's started seeing one of her coworkers at the bakery, and she's been spending a lot of time at his place. She hasn't slept in her bed or washed her face at her sink in days.

Dennis lives with two guys and they all have girlfriends, so there are six people occupying the apartment most of the time. It's small with a single bathroom and a single slim disc of gray bar soap in the tub. Everyone uses this soap to shower. Once there was a red hair around it, which would be from Elise, and once the soap still had bubbles on it when she picked it up. This morning, she washed her body with shampoo instead.

Dennis and his roommates and their girlfriends are all heavy drinkers, and Karen's been drinking a lot to keep up. Her stomach is upset and her brain is misty. She needs a real shower. But she likes Bette's apartment, its wooden floors and big, open rooms. Everything is cleaner here than at her place, which, except for the soap, isn't better than Dennis's. Also, if Bette wakes up, she might pay Karen for the time she's been waiting.

The sound of televised golf drifts from the back rooms. In his down-time, Andy watches sports and reads biographies of politicians. According to Bette, he was briefly a professional football player. Karen told Dennis this when she was describing the job.

"What position?" Dennis said. It was a slow afternoon at the bakery. They were sitting behind the counter, eating buns.

"I don't know. I think he spent a lot of time on the bench."

"Watch out for him."

"What do you mean?"

"Football." Dennis paused as though he might leave it at that. "It's violent."

This made no sense. "How many football players do you know?"

"I don't know any. That isn't an accident."

"Andy seems very gentle."

Dennis frowned. He walked over to the cooling rack and began emptying a sheet of cookies onto a glass display tray.

Andy really is gentle. He once put his hand on Karen's hip to step around her; it was like being brushed by a leaf. Another time Karen walked into the television room while he was having a salad. There were a few sprouts on his fork and he chewed and chewed before taking another bite. Mindful eating. Oprah or somebody had done a segment on it. A thin, old doctor said that everyone should take more time to taste their salmon, berries, whatever. But Andy probably doesn't call it mindful eating.

Karen's seen Andy smile to himself and once she caught him humming, as if even his inner world were peaceful. He's so thin Karen was surprised when Bette mentioned the football career.

"Isn't he small for that?" she said.

"It was ages ago," Bette said.

How long ago, Karen still wonders. How old is Andy? At first she wanted to know because she was attracted to him, but soon her desire wore itself out on his shyness, his reserve. Also, Dennis appeared in her life. Now her interest is more detached. Who is this quiet man who spends his days in an old woman's house, watching golf, eating salad? Is he like the protagonist of Karen's novel? Is Bette his boxer?

Karen is almost asleep. Dark pools fill her mind. I have to see him, she thinks. Then, who? Andy? Dennis? She works her way back along her thoughts, but they're disconnected.

She doesn't want to nap here. That would be unprofessional. She opens her eyes. In the kitchen, as Andy promised, a rosy ham shank sits on the cutting board next to a long, sharp knife. Karen slices a couple of pieces and puts them on a plate with water crackers and blue cheese from the refrigerator. She hasn't been eating well. Dennis is a vegetarian and his roommates are vegan, but more profoundly their diet consists of not eating much at all. Dennis skips breakfast, has a roll or muffin in the afternoon and then eats a late, light supper. Karen's pants are loose, which is nice, but an adjustment. She's had a headache for a week. Dennis says it's detox related, but Karen thinks it's from starvation.

She carries her plate back into the living room and tears a piece of ham with her fingers. It makes only a small dent in her hunger.

"You're an omnivore," Dennis once said. "I have no problem with that."

But he does have a problem with it.

"You shouldn't mix flesh and carbohydrates," he said last week, as he watched her eat a turkey sandwich. "It gets stuck in your colon."

When they had dinner at her friend's house and he was offered a piece of fish, he said, "I don't eat anything with eyes."

Flesh. Eyes. Karen doesn't want to think about it.

"Pretty good, huh?" Andy stands in the doorway. With his quiet footsteps, he often catches Karen by surprise. Now it's as though he's materialized out of nothing, out of her thoughts about Dennis and ham.

Karen looks at her plate.

"It came today in the mail," Andy says. "Danny sent it."

Danny and Martha are the children of Bette's late husband. Ethan was right, in a sense. Bette is mostly alone. She and her stepchildren don't get along. They haven't really spoken since Jerry died. But they write to Bette on holidays and occasionally one of them sends mail-order food. Last month she received a crate of grapefruit. She sometimes reciprocates and recently had Karen order six jars of tomato jelly from a jam maker in France.

"Where's it from?" she asks Andy.

"Michigan."

"All this food flying around. It's such a waste—the gas."

This is a thought she's had before, and one that went over well when she shared it with Dennis, but it doesn't interest Andy, and, actually, Karen doesn't know what resources are consumed when a ham shank travels from Michigan to New York. It could be one of those exceptions—like how it's better to ship an apple from New Zealand than drive one in from Washington. But that has to do with the virtues of shipping, and Karen doubts the ham came by boat.

"She's still sleeping," Andy says.

"Do you think she's OK?"

"She had a procedure the other day. She'll be up eventually. I'm heading home. You should too."

"I'm meeting someone up here at seven. I'll stick around until then."

This isn't the exact truth. Karen is seeing Dennis tonight but she doesn't know when, and they won't get together in Bette's neighborhood. She'll probably go to his house.

"Turn off the lights when you leave if you remember," Andy says. "But I'll be back in the morning so it's not a big deal."

"I'll turn them off."

"Actually, better keep a couple on, in case she wakes up."

"Sure."

Andy goes. Karen hears him zip his jacket, close the door. She doesn't like being in the apartment alone but still hopes Bette will wake and pay her.

This morning, as Karen was putting on her shirt, Dennis said, "You've been staying here a lot."

"I've been meaning to go home," Karen said.

"It's not that." Dennis pulled her back into the bed, curled next to her. This is one of the surprises about their relationship. He was almost aloof when they first met, but since they've started sleeping together he's been really affectionate. Karen touched his hair.

"I want you here *all* the time," Dennis said. "It's just the other girls—Molly and Elise—they chip in for heat and groceries. You've been having all your meals here."

Karen sat up. "Three. Three dinners."

"Yeah." Dennis was speaking softly, tugging on her arm, trying to pull her back down. "But food isn't free, right? You aren't going to stop coming, are you?"

That first night, Karen had thought about offering Dennis some money at the grocery store, but things have been tight recently. With what she makes at the bakery and at Bette's, she has just enough for rent and her own supplies. And the food served at

Dennis's was simple. Spaghetti, mashed potatoes, vegetarian baked beans. Nothing that would break the bank.

"I'll give you money," she said, pulling away from him. "Tonight. I have to get to an ATM."

"I didn't mean to upset you." He leaned on an elbow, gave her a concerned look.

"I'm not upset."

The confrontation made her think. Had he ever paid for her? No. The first time they went out together, she'd paid for him. They were at a bar, and he didn't have cash. "Would you spot me?" he'd said. He didn't like to pay the debit-card fees on principle, and because of the same principle, he didn't have a credit card.

There were other bad things about Dennis. He wore natural deodorant, and didn't change his shirts very often, so he smelled a little sour. And he was lazy. When things were quiet at the bakery, he'd put his head on the counter and close his eyes. Well, they have this in common. Karen is lazy too.

When Karen left Dennis's house this morning she thought she'd break up with him, but she's not sure. Dennis's cupboards are filled with pottery he made—cups and deep bowls. He made the wooden coffee table in his living room too, and just last weekend he helped Karen install bookshelves. The potatoes they'd eaten, he'd cooked them, and they were delicious. He's generous, just not with money. Dennis is cute and seems physically at ease—all his movements are assured. Best of all, he appears to really like Karen, even admire her. "You're smart," he'd said that night at the bar, listening to her talk about the book with the man and his jobs. She's been reading that book for a while. "What are you doing working at a bakery?"

What's Karen doing working at a bakery, working for Bette? What's she doing now, waiting in this apartment for an old woman who is asleep or—the thought is there whenever Bette naps—maybe dead? This is what you get, Karen's father would say, for not applying to law school. With part of her next paycheck, she'll pick up an LSAT book.

Now, though, the best plan is to leave. The quiet apartment makes her jumpy. Dennis will understand if she can't chip in right away. She'll remind him of the beers she covered. If you count those, they're probably even.

Karen goes into the kitchen to put away the ham. She makes noise with the tinfoil and shuts a drawer loudly, listening to see if it has woken Bette, but there isn't a sound from her room. She thinks, What if Bette *is* dead? What if she's dead and I just leave? Karen decides to check on her.

The hallway to Bette's room has wallpaper with a pattern of branches and berries. There's blue carpeting on the floor. Inside, the bedroom is brighter than the rest of the apartment. Andy didn't close the shades and light falls on the bed, its white duvet, the small mound on one side where Bette is lying. Karen stops with her hand on the door, tries to see the blanket rise and fall with Bette's breath.

She walks over. Bette is on her side, her mouth turned down. Karen puts her hand in front of Bette's nose and feels a haze of warm air. Bette turns her head.

"What are you doing?" Her eyes are small and aged—waxy, wrinkled lids, clouded irises—and her gaze is vague.

Karen thinks, She isn't going to pay me. "I'm leaving," she says. "I wanted to check—do you need anything?"

"You're late," Bette says.

"My shift changed. I've been here since four."

"Your shift." Bette puts a hand on the bed and drags herself into a sitting position. Her nightgown gaps open, revealing the reddish skin of her chest.

"Well," Karen says. "I'm going now." But she doesn't move because Bette has turned her head, and maybe she's looking for her wallet.

"Yes," Bette says, facing her again. "Go. Until next week, my dear."

Dennis doesn't pick up his phone. Karen will go home, take a shower, maybe go to sleep. The subway ride to her apartment is long, and she reads her book. The boxer and the man get along, form a bond. It's just like a news segment she saw. Prisoners were matched with abused dogs and they rehabilitated one another. The man in the book is well paid for his work because of how menacing the dog is to everyone else. His reputation grows and he finds other clients, one of whom he falls in love with. All this is packed into the last chapter. Maybe I should work with animals, Karen thinks. Dogs would be a little big; cats would be better, or guinea pigs. Karen tries to picture herself nursing a guinea pig back to health, but she can't remember what guinea pigs look like—something brown and furry and fat. Does anyone care when they get sick?

Or she could follow in Andy's footsteps, be a nurse to people. Karen's interest in Andy isn't completely detached. Sometimes she sees—tries to see—herself in him. They're both floating around Bette's apartment. But Karen doesn't have the temperament or the stomach to be a nurse.

A woman with a long braid has been looking at her, trying to catch her eye. Now she scoots toward her and Karen realizes the sweet smell in the car is this lady's perfume.

"I loved that book. I gave it to all my friends." The woman's shirt is inside out. There's a white tag on one side like a little flag. "Isn't it wonderful? I mean, inspiring?"

Karen smiles to mask her irritation. This person is trying to claim a relationship with her. That's what it feels like. She thinks of that first night with Bette—the girl. Something about Karen invites this. She's too accessible.

"It's pretty good," she says, but when the train stops at her station, she leaves the book in the car.

Over the weekend, she speaks to Andy.

"Can you tell her I'm not feeling well?"

"You OK?"

"Completely OK. I just don't know if I'm contagious."

"You'll be here Thursday?" says Andy, which makes Karen wish that she were there with them now.

"As soon as I'm better," she says.

CROWDED SKIES

Naturally, I see Max while I'm waiting to board. He's dragging a green rolling suitcase and smiling.

"Willa," he says. "What are you doing here?"

"Going to California." I smile too.

"That's where *I'm* going."

"Lizzie's wedding."

He nods.

Max and I split up a year ago and haven't been in touch. We'd been living in an apartment his parents bought for him in a neighborhood downtown, close to the water and a park. We had a good cheese place on our block, a cheap nail salon, and a fancy pet store. Max and I thought about getting one of their big dog beds, to use as a kind of lounging place.

"How did you get here?" he says. "The train?"

"Taxi."

"I could have given you a lift."

After I left, I kept hearing about the new women Max was sleeping with: a fact-checker at his magazine, a married person, an actress who was still a teenager. I'd left a lot behind when I moved. Not things that belonged to me in the sense that I'd *purchased* them—I took all of that with me. I left things that belonged to me in a different way—things I had used and lived with for a long time. These women were sleeping in my bed, on the violet sheets I convinced

Max to buy. They were washing in my shower, stepping out onto my fuzzy blue mat. They were eating cereal at my kitchen table from my red glass bowl and looking out the window, watching my neighbor herd his children down the block. They were wandering around my pet store, testing out the beanbag model. Or maybe they weren't doing that.

"This is kind of a pain, isn't it?" Max says.

"The wedding?"

"It's so far away. I had to take two days off work."

The wedding is in Berkeley, where Lizzie lives.

"Travel is expensive," I say.

"And the gift. Did you see the registry?"

"The plates." The plates are white with a garden pattern on the rim—grass, flowers, little ruby beetles. Each one costs hundreds of dollars.

"All those taupe towels."

"I think they chose good knives." But I don't enjoy this conversation. The phrases are slippery, worn-in. Everyone gossips about weddings. I have a daydreamy feeling, as though the better part of me has gone to sleep.

"Excuse me a sec," Max says, "I just remembered something."

He pulls out his phone and begins typing. I look at my ticket; the text dances before my eyes. I should be asleep—would be if I weren't going on this trip. I'm achy and keep catching a smell. Everyone in the terminal looks tired and grubby, everyone except Max. He rubs his eyes. He's drowsy in the clean way of a child. His breath probably smells like milk. His hair probably smells like hay. What a jerk.

"Sorry about that," he says. "I just"—he presses his mouth together—"I had to tell someone something."

I don't say anything.

"So we were—what were we—?"

"I'm going to sit," I say. "Want to sit?" There are a couple of empty chairs near us. The seams are split in a few places and some yellow foam is coming out.

"No," Max says. "No, thanks. I have to get my seat on the flight changed. I'm next to the bathroom."

"Good luck."

Max walks off, rolling his suitcase behind him. I think about calling one of my friends to complain about running into him, but it's still early, and it's no coincidence. I knew he was going to the wedding. Months ago, Lizzie told me he was invited.

"Are you OK with it?" she asked.

"Of course." I was visiting her. We were at a bakery near her place, eating yellow cake with raspberry jam and white frosting. Chalky rosettes were scattered over the top. I tried to eat one, and it hurt the roof of my mouth.

"If you aren't OK with it, tell me. You come first. I'm serious."

"You come first, Liz. It's your wedding."

Lizzie licked frosting off her spoon. "That's true. But you definitely come before Max."

This was a month after I'd moved, and I was still unhappy about some things. My new apartment was dirty. I shared it with two nice guys—polite, quiet. They'd both gone to Macalester and both worked for the city. They had girlfriends who sometimes invited me to join them when they went apple picking in New Jersey or to the water spa in Queens. I liked the girlfriends and I liked my roommates, but they were messy. They left wet towels on the couch and water glasses on every surface. The kitchen counter was covered with nearly empty beer cans. Sometimes the sight of my apartment made me angry. Other times I was frustrated because the subway was loud and crowded or because customers at the bookstore were impatient. And sometimes I was overcome with a dark, abandoned feeling because none of my friends were available to talk and it was night and I was by myself. Even when I wasn't upset about Max, I knew the situation with Max was the cause.

But I wouldn't ask Lizzie not to invite him. That would be humiliating. Also, Max and Lizzie's fiancé were friends. Brian might actually want him there.

I sit in my foam chair, looking at the sunny concrete yard where the planes wait, moving in their thick, slow way, as if the air around them is water. I watch them for a long time. There's a little truck weaving around them, like a minnow around whales. I place my bag on the seat next to me and put my head on it and fall asleep.

Eventually the gate opens and we sift on board. It's an old plane; it shifts and creaks while we get settled. "This plane is crap," Max says as he passes me on the way to his seat. When we start to move, it dips from side to side. People clutch the arms of their chairs. We pick up speed and it seems obvious something is wrong. I think, could this morning get any worse? But in a heavy way, like an old person getting out of a chair, we lift.

Max and I aren't the only wedding guests on the plane. There's also Kate, who worked with Lizzie at some point, sitting a couple rows in front of me. She has a gray blanket around her legs, and she's reading a gossip magazine, turning the pages slowly. I met her at the East Coast engagement party. She was drinking white wine at a small table in the back of the bar. Something had just happened to her. A person in her family was sick, or one of her friends, or her pet. Lizzie told me about it, but I can't remember. I'd had a few glasses of spiked mint lemonade. Max was at the party with the young actress, who did not, actually, look so young. I rolled pieces of my napkin and flicked them in her direction until Lizzie's friend Karen made me stop. The next day I called Karen to ask how badly I'd behaved. "Worse than anyone?" I said.

"Not close," Karen said.

"Top five percent?"

"No, no."

"Top fifty?"

"Maybe. *Maybe* top thirty. Everyone was drinking."

"Were you?"

"I wasn't, no. You should have some tea. Twig tea."

They won't serve twig tea on this plane, though air travel could use more of that—spa touches. The air in the cabin is stale and dry. The skin on my face is tight. Recently I've noticed creases around my eyes. Lizzie says they're from dehydration, that all I need to do is moisturize and drink more water. I take Vaseline out of my bag and ask for water from the flight attendant, whose skin is worse than mine—there's a flaky patch on his cheek. I'd offer him Vaseline but he's grumpy, keeps scolding people about their carry-ons.

"Give it to me," he says to people whose bags don't fit underneath the seats. "Here—to me."

He brings me a mini bottle with a plastic cup.

Carey is also on the flight, a few rows back. When I turn around, I see his leg extended into the aisle, the orange sole of his sneaker. At the beginning of college, he lived with a guy named Chase—both of them nice-looking and tall. They walked to class together, ate together in the dining hall. When they stopped spending so much time together, Carey lost some of his sparkle. I wonder what people think I've lost now that I'm not with Max. Well, I know what I've lost: soft sheets, a deep glass cereal bowl, a plan for a dog bed.

There were rumors about Chase. I heard he was distantly related to the British royal family, was seventy-something in line to the throne. Someone told me his aunt was connected to the mob in New York. Our sophomore year he started dating a grad student in the business school named Olivia. People said she was divorced and had a child. Someone told me that Chase and the child got along well, but Brian said Chase didn't like the child and was encouraging Olivia to give it back to the father. "Give it back to the father" was Brian's phrase.

"It's not a table," I said. "You can't give it back."

"I know," said Brian. "Just repeating what I heard."

Chase and Olivia lived in the apartment next to Max's one year. There was no sign of anyone else living there, so maybe she did give up custody, or maybe the child never existed. The walls were thin and Max and I would sometimes listen to them fight. At first I thought I was the only one, listening while I was studying or stirring vegetables for dinner. Then one morning Max mentioned something Olivia had said the night before—something about Chase being irresponsible. He left his clothes everywhere, kept losing his wallet, forgetting his keys. She always had to walk back to the apartment to let him in, always in the worst weather—the snow, the rain.

"Maybe he had so much trouble with the kid because *he* wants to be a kid," Max said.

"You still think there's a kid?" I said.

After that, we listened together. We listened while we got dressed in the morning and over dinner. We listened as if Chase and Olivia were a book on tape or a radio soap. Their fights began with a specific complaint—the clothes, Olivia's friendship with one of her professors—and then broadened: how tired they were of the whole relationship.

"Did you say you're done?" Olivia said one night. "Is that what you said?"

"What I said is I'm almost done."

"What does that mean?"

"I'm close to being done."

"Thank you for the explanation, asshole."

They often called each other asshole. Max said it was probably how they made introductions: "This is my asshole boyfriend, Chase." But they didn't break up.

Max and I did, though we rarely fought and were mostly polite when we did. I once threw a pillow across the room. It knocked over a glass, which fell and spilled seltzer onto the rug, but didn't break. I wished it had. If it had, I thought, this irritating weight in my stomach might have broken up too. But afterward, the whole thing seemed embarrassing. Lizzie told me it was OK. "You probably should have thrown it at him," she said.

The flight doesn't serve food, but I've brought a bagel and unwrap it at the halfway point. The woman sitting next to me is eating grain salad out of Tupperware. She's wearing pink pants and has creamy skin. She's engrossed in a boxing movie on the tiny screen in front of her and she throws a couple punches along with the characters. She would've thrown the pillow at Max.

When we broke up, my father came to help me move. Max was staying with his brother in Philadelphia, and my dad and my friend Caroline met me at my apartment to pack and load my things into a U-Haul.

"This is quite a place," my dad said. It was on the first floor and there was a small tiled patio in the back. When we moved in it had been summer, and we sat out there every night drinking beer mixed with ginger ale or Prosecco, and I thought it was great being an adult. Max's parents were making the mortgage payments; we were only responsible for the maintenance.

When I left it was summer again, the kind of heat that makes sitting and standing feel like exercise. I was sweating in unfamiliar places—my calves, the tops of my arms.

"It's purifying," Caroline said. She was pulling strands of denim off her frayed shorts.

"Use scissors." I handed her the sharp pair we kept in the take-out-menu drawer.

It took us four hours to pack. Caroline kept suggesting things we could do to Max. "Someone told me about this: in winter, we break into his car and stitch a dead fish into the backseat. It won't smell until the summer, and then it will never stop smelling."

Which brought to mind something else I was losing: the car. "I don't want to punish him," I said.

"But you're so depressed," said Caroline.

"Not *so*. A little." Because moving was jarring, but destroying Max's stuff wouldn't help. I wanted Max's things—my things—to remain intact.

When we had everything packed, it only took up a small portion of the space in the truck.

"We could have done this in a cab," my dad said. "I had a feeling."

Max comes to see me near the end of the flight. He kneels in the aisle and leans in, our faces close.

"So are you bringing anyone?" he asks. "A date. To the wedding."

"No," I say. "Are you?"

"I wasn't going to but this girl—it's kind of serious. It's who I was texting earlier?" He shakes his hand in the air, his fingers clasped around an invisible phone.

The woman sitting next to me, the one in the pink pants, looks at Max and I can see her register his behavior.

I say, "Where is she?"

"On a later flight."

There's an announcement about choppy air. Everyone must sit down, fasten seatbelts.

"So," Max says. "Where are you staying? Want to split a cab?"

"Sure," I say, but we probably won't. I'll have to wait for my duffel at the luggage carousel; Max found space for his big rolling bag on the plane. He doesn't care about angry flight attendants. He hates to check luggage; he's very impatient generally.

I never thought I'd meet a spouse in college. I didn't know anyone thought that until I got there.

"I walk around," one boy said to me, "thinking, will it be you? Will it be you?"

"Like that game where you have to guess who the murderer is," I said.

"I guess." He thought for a moment. "No, not really."

Even when I started dating Max, we'd been together for a year, then two years, and then three, and even when we moved in together, I didn't think we'd get married. Max seemed to think so. Once when we were out with Lizzie's friends, Karen started talking about her cousin's wedding, where ice cream had been served with candy spoons. Max said, "We should get that."

"For what?" I asked.

Just before we broke up, he said, "Where is this going?"

"I don't understand that question," I said. "How can you know where anything is going?"

He said, "Let's talk about where it is."

Then he said, "I don't know if you were ever happy being with me."

I said that wasn't true, although I'd sometimes wondered the same thing. But in the following weeks, it seemed I *had* been happy with Max. Without him, I was miserable. Did people released from bad relationships lose their appetites? Even for their favorite food—avocado? Even for simple food—cereal? Did they walk around hunched over as though it were cold, when it was really hot? My colleague at the bookstore said they did. He said that even if you could barely stand to be in the same room with a person, you could miss that person like crazy. He said this and then said he wished we kept liquor in the back—why shouldn't we all have a drink at the end of the night?—and then he asked me to alphabetize the *m*'s.

I know how this weekend will go. Lizzie's sent me the schedule several times. There's a pig roast tonight and a baseball game tomorrow morning and then the ceremony at five. Lizzie is wearing cream, like antique paper, her mother is wearing shimmering blue, like tropical waters, Karen and I are wearing green, like new grass. Karen says it's more like pea soup. At the reception we'll eat short ribs and cake. We'll drink one glass of champagne but unlimited wine. I'll get a stomachache. Karen and I will go back to our hotel room and try to find something to watch on Lifetime and the next day Karen will make me walk outside so we can clear our heads. We'll stop at the brunch to say good-bye to the families. Lizzie's mother will hug me; she always smells like flowers and soap. Then I'll be flying home.

The landing—no surprise—is bumpy. When we hit the ground, we bounce several times and seem to speed up. I think of Max's kind of serious girlfriend. She could be boarding her flight at this very moment, in a new plane, leaping into windless skies. Wherever she is, she's probably well rested. I wonder if she spent the night at Max's. I wonder if she's made friends with the lady at the bagel place. My bagel place. Actually I have a new bagel place, and the people who work there are nice—they give me free coffee all the time. The plane bumps again and seems to sway across the runway. This is it, I think, but it isn't.

OPEN ROAD

They were driving north to the town where Peter grew up. They'd been in the car for three hours and outside the land was broadening around them. There were soft hills, shallow valleys, a few small houses.

"Hey," said Peter. "The mountains are purple."

"Oh?"

"Look at them."

Karen glanced out the window.

"My side."

She looked the other way, moving her head carefully. The mountains were layered like a diorama. Filmy clouds swam around their peaks. They were nice mountains, not so different from others she'd seen.

She turned back to the road. If Peter knew her better he wouldn't ask her to look in every direction like this, and if she knew him better she wouldn't do it even if he did ask. Karen had motion sickness and in cars she only looked straight ahead. But Peter was still getting to know her and she wanted to make a good impression.

"Like being out West," she said.

"Yeah. They're like—have you been to Colorado?"

She said she'd been to Utah.

"I went kayaking in Colorado," Peter said and told a story about a long day on a river. He got the peeling kind of sunburn, a fish chased his boat, and he and his friend rescued a cat when it leaped from its owner's raft. "Andre jumped in. The lady was so grateful."

"Did you get a reward?"

"We were thirsty, but she didn't have water so she gave us some grapes."

Karen used to keep grapes in the freezer; they turned into icy little candies. Why had she stopped doing that? She said, "Anyway that's refreshing."

Peter said it wasn't—the grapes were soft and warm. "Andre liked them," he said. "Grapes make my mouth itch."

"Couldn't you drink the river?"

"No, no. Giardia."

"Actually, my mother had that once." She saw her mom, years ago, pale and sweaty on the couch, and felt a rush of distress. Of course her mother was fine now. "There'd been beavers in the pond that summer."

Peter said, "That would do it."

Karen owed all this to Amanda, who had set them up. Amanda and Karen worked for a conservation organization. Karen had applied to the job after a very dull day at the bakery where she used to work. She'd sent in her resume not expecting to hear anything back, but Siri—now her boss—had written the next day. Amanda had been present for the interview.

"How are you working with difficult people?" she'd asked.

"What a question!" said Siri.

Karen never found out whom Amanda meant. It could have been one of her not-so-funny jokes. Everyone at the organization was pleasant and Siri, in particular, was a dream to work for. She never let Karen stay past six and she sometimes brought her gifts—lightly worn shoes, chocolates from the duty-free shop at the airport, an old rice cooker after Karen mentioned that she couldn't get the timing right. Some people had a cool and detached relationship to presents. Not Karen—she loved them. The good working conditions made up for the poor salary and the fact that she didn't have much experience with conservation, was even new to personal conservation efforts, like recycling. "You can't recycle that," Amanda was always saying when she dropped something into the plastics bin. "It's the wrong type."

Though Amanda was younger than Karen, she'd become a sort of workplace older sibling to her, and recently Karen had been complaining about the guys she met—quiet and serious.

"*You're* quiet and serious," Amanda said. They were sitting in Amanda's cubicle, looking at pictures of the vacation she'd taken in Mexico with friends.

"I'm not so serious," said Karen, straightening up. Amanda had lovely posture—she floated around the office. Perched on her chair, she looked like her muscles were lightly engaged, like she could stand easily at any moment. Karen found this inspiring.

"Maybe not deep down," Amanda said. "But you seem serious because you're so quiet."

"No. Deep down I am serious, but something gets—people don't think I'm serious."

"Hm." Amanda returned her attention to the computer.

Karen took a Hershey's Kiss from the bowl on her desk. "I've had the most success dating people who are different from me." She wondered if this were true. The last person she'd been with was Dennis, from the bakery. He wasn't like her and wasn't serious either. Sullen at times, but not serious. He was a wizard with potatoes. Karen missed him, but not too much.

Amanda, facing the computer, examining a photo of her profile bathed in sunlight, said, "Everyone thinks they want to meet someone different, but that's just an escape."

"Well, what's wrong with escape?" said Karen, full of conviction. Amanda always did this—stuck to her position. You couldn't budge her. She had her serene, unbothered demeanor, but underneath she was a mule. "What if what you're escaping is not so great?"

"That's not what we're talking about," Amanda said. "What you want to escape is you. And you, by whom I mean everyone, or no one. No one can do that." She stopped clicking her mouse, gave her head a toss, like she was shaking off the pronouns. She faced Karen and said, "You can *never* escape yourself," and sped through photos of a few women wearing sombreros at a bar, pausing on an image of a pale stone structure. "Here's Tulum, where I got heat stroke."

Later that afternoon she handed Karen a piece of paper with Peter's number on it and promised they were nothing alike.

"Oh no." Karen put the paper on her desk. "I can't call."

Amanda scowled, but Karen didn't acknowledge it. That weekend he called her.

And now they were on the road. Peter's car was an old green sedan. It smelled like tobacco and cinnamon and had a warm, lived-in feeling. Karen smoothed the furry blue fabric of her seat. Outside, it had started to rain.

"I hope it doesn't rain the whole weekend," Peter said.

Karen said "me too," though she hoped it would. Peter had planned a bike ride, but they wouldn't go if it kept raining. Karen had let Peter think she enjoyed biking. "I love bikes," she'd said, after he'd told her that he sometimes biked to work. At the time she'd been remembering all the nice things about bicycling—how it created a breeze when there wasn't a breeze, how easy it was when you went downhill. But Karen hadn't been on a bike since she was eight, and now she was caught up with all the bad things about them—how difficult it was to turn, how frightening when a car went by, how tiring the whole experience could be for your legs.

"If it rains we can do other stuff," she said. "We could go on a house tour."

"You wouldn't get to see the waterfall. We'd be all cooped up."

"That's true." Karen scratched Peter's arm. "That would be too bad."

They met for the first time at the botanical gardens because Karen wanted to see the droopy roses, the ones beginning to brown.

"That's like going out on Valentine's Day," Amanda said.

"It's not about romance," Karen said. "I like how they collapse."

She found him by the ticket booth and was surprised by how tall he was—her head barely reached his shoulders. He was wearing a royal-blue T-shirt. He said, "So. I think this will be fun."

He'd used a similar phrase on the message—that it would be fun to get together, that he thought they would have fun. His tone suggested that the idea of them having fun was amusing, maybe because it was so unlikely. Karen took a brochure and tried unsuccessfully to locate the roses. It didn't matter—they were just behind the gate, arranged in long, stately lanes.

But when they were among the plants, she wasn't sure what to do. The flowers didn't do much. Karen said, "The roses they sell at the supermarket are nothing like this. They all look like plastic." She often bought supermarket flowers, but that wasn't important.

Peter was in front of a plant with lots of yellow blossoms. "My mom likes this kind," he said.

"Yellow?"

"Anything but red."

They stayed at the park for half an hour, not speaking much, looking around, though Karen wasn't taking things in. Her nerves were making it hard to focus. The roses and Peter's blue shirt and the white stone path were flashing in her vision in pieces. She steadied her gaze on the space above Peter's shoulder and asked whether he was hungry. He said he was not at the moment, but he wouldn't mind eating. Then he said he might be hungry by the time they reached a restaurant. Finally he said, "I am a little hungry."

They went to a café nearby with small wooden tables and an aging wait staff. Karen, who had recently begun to notice the looks of much older men, decided their waiter must once have been very handsome. He was handsome now. He had a military appearance—short, compact, good posture. Karen had worked at a restaurant one summer and had slept with one of her colleagues there. This waiter was more or less an older, better-looking version of that one. He took a pad out of his green miniapron and looked at them without saying anything.

"Bloody Mary," Karen said.

"Two," said Peter.

"Sure thing," the waiter said.

Karen thought, What would it be like to date *him*, a man of few words? What if she'd gotten everything backward?

The drinks came out garnished with celery and toothpicks stacked with olives and after a few sips, Karen was having fun. Not only that, she was able to look at Peter directly. He had a precise jawline and thick eyelashes. He was draped over his chair—the opposite of Amanda's posture, but equally graceful.

"You have elegant hands," he said.

She'd been twirling a toothpick. Her hands did look nice—clean and neat. She brought them back into her lap with a hoarding feeling, as if they were possessions. "Thank you."

"Giving you compliments is satisfying," Peter said. "It's like throwing a baseball into a mitt. It makes a nice thwack."

They were both drunk when they went back to his apartment. On his windowsill was a row of succulents, thriving in their stone pots. Of course, Karen thought, succulents require little care. There was a blue fleece on his bed—the same blue as his shirt. He put his hand up her blouse and started to unbutton her pants, but she stopped him. They'd just met. When his roommate came home, she said she had to leave.

"So?" said Amanda, in the office the next day.

"Well, he's great." Karen was working her way through a mini box of raisins. She didn't want to talk to Amanda about the date. "He's so tall."

"He is."

"He has really nice plants."

"Pants?"

"Plants."

"He has plants?"

"Succulents. I think the key with those is to not be overzealous in your attention."

"What are you talking about?"

"I don't know." Karen shook the last clump of raisins onto her desk. "I thought he was—I think we had a nice time. I think we'll get together again." Her fingers were sticky. "I have to wash my hands."

And here they were, heading away from the city, toward—Karen didn't know what. Not a suburb, not exactly the country, a town, Peter had said. It had stopped raining and Karen was a bit sick, as if a small organ had come loose and was drifting around her midsection.

Peter was a good driver, though. He rested one hand casually on the lower bend of the wheel. He was like one of those superior dog trainers who only have to look at an animal to make it obey. Karen didn't have a license, but she wasn't impressed by the way most people drove. Ethan, her old boyfriend, would talk himself through each truck they passed. "I'm passing you, truck," he'd say. "On your left. No big deal." Often he couldn't pass at all and they'd follow the trucks for long stretches. Ethan told Karen that if a car and a truck had an accident, there was a 90 percent chance that the people in the car would die. Peter seemed to have no trouble passing trucks, even the long ones.

"Did you know that if a car and a truck have an accident, there's a ninety percent chance the people in the car will die?" Karen said.

Peter grimaced. "What about the person in the truck?" he said. "What are his odds?"

Karen mulled this over. "I don't know."

"It's a dangerous job. I read about it in the *Times* Magazine. They're all extremely sleep deprived, hopped up on drugs, among other things."

For their second date, they'd gone to a Greek restaurant.

"It's known for its moussaka," Peter said.

"Perfect," said Karen, though she didn't like eggplant. She ordered grilled fish and drank three gin and tonics. Peter told her about his job as a high school math teacher.

"The other week a student punched me," he said.

"You're kidding. Where did he punch you?"

"She. My shoulder."

"What did you do?"

"Sent her to the principal's office. She was suspended. I still feel bad about it."

"It wasn't your fault." Karen put her hand on his forearm.

"She didn't hit me hard."

Peter said he was considering quitting. He thought he wasn't cut out to work with adolescents. "I'm not sensitive enough," he said.

"Maybe you're too sensitive," said Karen, liking this idea. "It bothers you too much."

"I've never worked so much in my life."

After dinner they went to her apartment. She'd cleaned earlier in anticipation of this, but walking in she saw a pair of underwear on her desk and her bank statement unfolded on the bed, so some kind of self-sabotage was at work. But the gin saved her; it allowed her to feel separate from the mess. The point was not what happened, but how you handled what happened. The trick, as people had been telling her for years and years, was to act like you didn't care. She picked up the statement and placed it over the underpants.

She unbuttoned Peter's shirt with a feeling of anticipation. With his long limbs and slightly round stomach, his easy way of reclining on the bed, he was a little glamorous. She felt shabby in comparison. She was with someone more beautiful than herself and was filled with humility and respect. She wouldn't be on top.

They'd been in the car for a long time. Hours and hours. The East Coast was enormous. Karen had known this—she'd seen it on a map—but it was the kind of thing you had to experience to fully understand. Karen's body felt attached to her seat, as if the seat were now an extension of her, another layer. The new order was skeleton, skin, seat. She still didn't feel well.

They crested a hill and met a stretch of glimmering taillights. "Accident," said Peter. They inched along next to a trailer with the word "milk" inscribed on its side in looping script. Karen remembered a large bin of orange juice at the restaurant where she'd worked. The first time she saw it, on the kitchen floor, she didn't recognize it.

"What is that?" she'd asked the chef.

"Orange juice," the chef said. "For the mimosas."

She thought of the bottom of the bin, the thin plastic separating the juice for the mimosas from the floor. She nudged the bin with her foot and the surface of the orange juice rippled. "What are you doing?" the chef said. "Don't do that."

Karen touched Peter's shoulder and pointed to the milk trailer. "Imagine if *that* truck got into an accident," she said. "All the milk on the highway."

"A lake of milk," Peter said, then frowned. "I used to love milk, but I can't drink it anymore. I'm lactose intolerant."

"Oh," Karen said. "I am too." She wasn't in the biological sense, but she thought the idea of milk was disturbing.

"Do you drink soy? There's this hemp stuff I like, the kind in the red box."

"I use soy." In fact she put cow's milk in coffee, and in cereal sometimes. Milk wasn't bad when it was mixed with things. It was a glass of plain milk that seemed strange. She couldn't get into it. If she talked too much, she might throw up. She put her head against the window, like she was going to sleep. How many true things had she said to Peter since they'd met? Not so many. At the moment, this was comforting, as if her real self was hidden somewhere out of the way.

The day after they slept together he called her. They went to the park and sat against a tree. The weather had changed; the air was light and clear. It made the summer air seem like it had been something else: fog or water. Peter talked about himself and rubbed Karen's wrist, where she thought she had an overuse injury from her keyboard. He said his father was taking painting classes and his mother had a job that required her to travel to California and France. Karen didn't catch what the job was. Something in food, maybe. She was only half listening, trying not to be bothered by the feeling of her tendons shifting under Peter's thumb. She imagined him at his most attractive—standing in front of a classroom, watering his succulents with a coffee mug. He said that in high school he'd been on the soccer team, but then a guy he didn't like joined, and he quit. The new guy had started seeing his ex, or he was seeing the new guy's ex, or they were both seeing each other's exes. Whatever the arrangement, jealousy was involved.

"When my high school boyfriend and I broke up," Karen said, "he started seeing someone who looked just like me from behind."

"Really," said Peter.

"You couldn't tell us apart."

Peter said that after he quit soccer, he started peak bagging.

Karen shifted away from the tree so she could face him. "What's that?"

"Oh," said Peter. "Just hiking."

She called her friend Danny, who lived in Utah. He was a ski instructor in the winter and a camp counselor in the summer. When he'd lived in New York, Karen watched the Olympics at his apartment. He had a soft, messy beard. Once they'd almost kissed, or something, but then hadn't, which made it embarrassing to remember.

Still, they kept in touch and he explained peak bagging to her. "They climb high mountains," he said. A set of high mountains—maybe all the mountains in a certain area above a certain elevation, maybe all those mountains in a certain amount of time. "Some people just call it bagging."

"That's a terrible name," Karen said.

"Who's this person?"

"A teacher."

Danny started telling Karen about his new girlfriend. "She has long hair. And she makes life seem so simple. She never worries about anything."

"Do you worry much?"

"Not too much. But sometimes I feel overwhelmed."

Overwhelmed was how *she* felt. "With what?"

"You know." There was a pause and Karen imagined him lying down. "All the stuff I'm doing, all the stuff I'm not doing."

Spending so much time with a person, eventually you stop caring what he thinks of you. Karen was irritated with Peter for taking her on this endless drive. Was he so handsome? She looked over. He was.

At last the traffic loosened and they moved faster. They passed a couple of cars at odd angles on the shoulder.

"Accident," Peter said. "Like I said."

Thinking about Peter bagging peaks gave Karen a queasy feeling. Her father used to take her skiing every winter and there would be guys on the mountain. At the time they'd been older than her. Now, they'd be much younger. They wore bright jackets—orange, red, blue—and sunglasses; well, they wore what everyone else wore. It was their attitude. They were always jumping around, always on the brink of falling. Sometimes they did fall, taking down a person or people or whole rope lines with them. But they were impatient with everyone else's mistakes. They glared at you if you hesitated, for example, at the entrance to the woods. Was Peter this type of person?

Peter claimed he didn't bag peaks any longer. "Mostly I just go on walks," he said.

Here's how it happened: he sent her an e-mail. *My parents are going away. Want to get out of the city?* Karen liked how he wrote it. It was the kind of thing she could imagine him saying in high school, when he'd been on the soccer team. But she wasn't sure she wanted to go.

"Why not?" Amanda asked. "Peter is cute and actually he's a really good guy." She said it as though she might easily have set Karen up with a bad guy.

"I'm not sure we see eye to eye," said Karen.

They were eating lunch at a deli near their office. Amanda sprinkled salt onto a hard-boiled egg. "You wanted someone different."

"I told him I like to bike."

"Everyone lies at first. Everyone does."

Karen scraped tuna salad off her sandwich. "I don't think he knows me at all."

"Well, of course not. Just clue him in gradually."

They were off the highway. Karen rolled down her window a little. Outside it smelled like soil and grass.

"The last girl I dated was pathologically arachnophobic," Peter said.

"Are all phobias pathological?" said Karen.

"I don't know. But when this girl saw a spider she'd have to leave the apartment."

"That it's a phobia implies that it's outside of normal behavior, right?"

"She'd be out of the building for hours."

"Jeez."

"Sorry." Peter looked over at her. "I know you aren't meant to talk about exes."

"I don't mind. I'm curious." All Amanda had known about Peter's romantic history was that he once went out with a woman who didn't wear shoes outside. "What was her name?"

"Annabelle," Peter said. "Actually she wasn't bad. She had a lisp and nice long hands. Kind of like yours." He winked.

"What happened?"

"She moved. Grad school. But it was ending anyway. We were on different paths. Hey, we're getting really close. We're closing in."

Still, he decided to stop to fill up the car. They were almost out of gas, and he thought Karen might have to pee. She didn't, but she went to the bathroom. She checked her face, expecting it to be broken out, or dry, something to reflect all the time on the road. But she looked the same as always, maybe a little wan.

Carsickness was always worse in the moments after you left the car. Karen thought about throwing up—she'd always done it easily. But Peter was buying bread and things right on the other side of the bathroom door. He might hear. So instead she tried to pee. And then, to extend her time in the bathroom, which she was sort of enjoying, she called Amanda.

"What's up?" said Amanda.

"We're at a pit stop. I'm in the bathroom."

"Oh. I'm about to go out. The theater in my neighborhood is doing that marathon. You're missing it. You're in the bathroom?"

"We've been in the car for ages. We had practically nothing to talk about."

"I'm not—" The connection was scratchy. Amanda was probably in the stairwell. There were fuzzy sounds and then Amanda said, clearly, "Do you want to leave? Come home?"

Karen hadn't considered going home. If she were home, she'd be in bed watching a movie, or heading out with Amanda, or having coffee with another friend. She wouldn't feel sick—that was almost certain. She leaned on the door. "Maybe I do want to go home."

"Well, I don't know *how* you're going to do that."

"But I don't *really* want to go home. I just wanted to talk to you—to talk to somebody without all the pressure." Which was what she'd wanted, and, to that end, it had been a mistake calling Amanda, who was always trying to get to the bottom of things.

"Where are you anyway?" Amanda said.

"I don't know. Somewhere north."

"It's spooky up there."

"We aren't getting any radio stations."

"Well." Amanda paused, as though she were waiting for Karen to say something, but Karen didn't know what to say. "Good luck," said Amanda.

Outside, Karen felt better. A breeze came by—it was refreshing. The time in the bathroom had done her good. The nausea was almost gone. She didn't want to go home, to leave Peter. People were always taking things too far, telling you to do something, when, most of the time, there wasn't anything to do.

Still, she wanted to say something to him, maybe something revealing. In the past, she'd gone about this in the wrong way. She'd spent a long time trying to talk to Dennis, for example, about her parents' divorce, which she was too young to remember. Dennis seemed to enjoy these conversations—he was eager to dig in—but they never went anywhere.

Back in the car, she said, "Rest-stop bathrooms can be iffy."

Peter raised his eyebrows. "I know."

"Yes. You never know what you're getting into. But that one was clean."

"I'll keep that in mind."

"Yes." And because she was on a roll, she said, "I'm not so attached to biking." They passed a tree with yellow leaves and Karen thought of the roses.

Peter said, "Oh—I thought you wanted to."

"But with the rain."

"We don't have to. We can do whatever."

Karen tried to make her face look neutral—not too excited, not relieved—but she must have overcorrected because Peter said, "What's wrong?"

"Nothing," she said, surprised that this was true.

SAM

A bowling alley opened on my block a few months ago, on the first floor of an old granite building. To create the space for it they joined a few storefronts together, one of which was my old Laundromat. The Laundromat made a stretch of the sidewalk smell like Tide. Now the closest laundry place is three blocks away, and the street smells like disinfectant. It's not a regular bowling alley—the kind people take their kids to, the kind that opens during the day and closes at night. It's a bowling alley and a nightclub. It plays thumping music, and its lights make the street look purple. I'm losing sleep.

My boyfriend, Lewis, suggested that I try to have it closed. "*Do* something," he said. "Make a change." Lewis thinks interrupting a person's sleep is a crime. "It is actually a torture technique," he said.

"I don't need it completely shut down," I said. "I wouldn't want people to lose their jobs."

"What about your pals at the Laundromat?"

The Laundromat was owned by an old couple who watched talk shows all day. The man was missing one of his thumbs. The woman wrote down all the orders by hand—her capitals took up three notebook lines. They were not warm, but they were reliable. The man lifted the clanking shutter at seven every morning. I heard they retired to Arizona.

"I think they left voluntarily," I said.

"Still," Lewis said.

"I might ask them to tone it down."

I stopped by that night to speak to the manager. A slim bald man wearing all black who said he was the bartender and the manager claimed not to have any control over the volume of the music or the brightness of the lights. "It's all preset." He said they'd bothered him too at first but that he'd grown accustomed to them. "Just like the rest of the city. The traffic and sirens and whatnot."

I said the situation was different. "People are supposed to enjoy the atmosphere here."

"Look around you."

The people around me looked happy. Near one lane, everyone was laughing. Another group was involved in a round of toasts. "No, wait," said a lady, turning to another. "To Melanie." The woman called Melanie dipped her head. She was wearing a scarf—deep blue, like a slice of ocean.

"Mel." The first person raised a nearly empty glass. "To you."

They were having a good time, which made it worse.

"Anyway," said the bartender-manager. "You'll have to talk to the guys at the home office." He told me there were two home offices—one in Texas and one in North Carolina.

"Is one like a summer home office?" I said.

"Yeah, good one. And good luck getting them on the phone."

I started to leave, but I think he felt badly because he called out, "Stop by sometime." Then he jogged over and handed me a green sheet of paper that entitled me to two mojitos for the price of one. I put it in my wallet. Lewis and I love mojitos.

I left messages in North Carolina and Texas and sent an email to the customer-service address for the parent company. It was called Candlelight, a strange name for an organization with a lighting strategy so at odds with the soft, soothing light of candles. Lewis and I spent a long time trying to find the right wording for the e-mail and finally settled on: *Would it be possible to please lower the volume of the music and dim the lights.* The next day I received a reply from somebody named Sam, the head of customer relations. *Hey Leila!* Sam wrote, and I felt startled to see my name. He said he was processing my comment and would respond fully in three weeks, but it's been over six weeks and Sam hasn't written again.

Lewis, meanwhile, began an Internet search for city bureaus that I could complain to. He started a list and was going to make the calls with me, but now Lewis is on a sit and can't help. He and a dozen or so other people are meditating in a room in the Berkshires. They sit for eight hours a day, with a break for lunch.

"It's magical," Lewis said, after the first time he went. "You're sitting there, cramped and miserable, and then—something happens."

"What happens? You relax?"

"I can't describe it. But it's true I'm more relaxed now. Like I've noticed that all the tiny muscles in my face, which are usually really tight—you know, around my jaw?" He touched the corners of his jaw. "Have you ever massaged your jaw?"

"They're loose, those muscles?"

"Not *loose.* Looser."

We were having dinner in a crowded restaurant. Lewis had the beginning of a beard and his skin was a healthy, burnished brown.

I said, "You look tan."

"The weather was incredible. We ate our meals in the field."

Lewis is suited to eating in a field. His body always seems too big for indoor spaces. At the restaurant I couldn't see his chair, except for when he leaned forward to take a piece of bread.

"What does the room where you sit look like? What color are the walls? I want to picture it."

"It used to be a school." Lewis twirled his spoon in his beet soup, like he could conjure the image there. "That was a long time ago, but think of an old schoolroom."

I had an image of a classroom from a movie or book. The floors were wooden and the desks were made of metal and nailed to the floor. The air was dusty. "Are there desks?"

"No. We sit on the floor on these amazing cushions."

I sit on the floor when I make my phone calls to the city departments. My apartment has parquet floors and I lean against the edge of my armchair and trace the pattern of the parquet with my toes while I'm on hold. Three strokes across, three strokes down. The hold music for some of the departments isn't bad—classical piano, Debussy and Chopin. I get into a rhythm and it's kind of like a sit, I think. Meditative movement. I tell this to Lewis one night when he calls, but he says, apologetically, that what I'm describing is not a sit. "Waiting for something," he says. "I think it's different. But I'm glad you're enjoying it."

The frustrating thing about the long hold times is that so far they haven't led to real people. After the music plays for a while, an answering machine picks up. "Please leave a detailed message," the machine says, so I recite the details of my situation—when the bowling alley opened, how loud the music is, how the lights make my block even less dark than other city blocks, which are not perfectly dark to begin with. And I give my personal details, my name and telephone number, which I say twice. I've left two messages for my district councilman and one for the borough president. At this point, I would be happy to receive just an acknowledgement of my calls, like what Sam from Candlelight sent—something to mark the fact that they happened.

When Lewis is on a sit I spend more time at work. I go in half an hour early and leave half an hour late. I catch up on my filing and try to do everything better. I work for an academic publisher whose main office is in London. I send and receive contracts and every so often I call academics to ask where their contracts are. Some of our authors are elderly and reclusive. They don't have e-mail accounts and they call me young lady and misplace contracts all the time. Right now we're waiting for a contract back from someone who is writing a history of the wool industry in the British Isles. Sheep and things like that. I've left messages at his house, but he hasn't responded.

My colleague Ethan has the same job I have, and he and I share a cubicle wall. At first we walked around the wall to talk, but recently we realized that wasn't necessary. Sitting at our desks we can easily hear each other, so we've started speaking through the wall. There are many benefits to this. I don't worry about having the right expression on my face when Ethan is talking, and I don't wonder whether he's feigning interest when I'm talking. We can behave naturally without offending each other.

Ethan spends a lot of time complaining about his wife, Elizabeth. They've been together since college, where they worked at the same library, but they were married recently and according to Ethan the first years of marriage are tremendously difficult no matter how long you've dated or even lived together.

"With every problem it's like, have I signed up for this for the rest of my life," he says.

Some of the problems—Elizabeth pestering him about installing a closet door—seem unlikely to last a lifetime. Others might. There are a few I'm not sure how to categorize. Once he was worried about Elizabeth's fidelity because she joked with the guy at the health food store.

"They joke?" I said.

"They have one about vitamin B."

"Have you put in the door?" Because he should have a door on his closet.

"Not yet. I have my eye on a beauty. It has these slats, like shutters?"

"Sounds perfect."

"It's a little pricey."

Recently the problems with Elizabeth have had to do with celiac disease. She was recently diagnosed. She's eliminated gluten from her diet and wants Ethan to do the same, in support.

"She won't let me have oatmeal," he says. "And she doesn't even like oatmeal."

"They have gluten-free oats," I say.

"I can't buy special versions of things—it ruins it."

"You could have rice. You could have quinoa."

Ethan says he doesn't want rice or quinoa.

"You can have oatmeal here."

"Eating breakfast at work is depressing."

"Listen. A bowling alley just moved into my neighborhood."

I tell him about the lights, the music, the poor sleep. I mention the bartender-manager and the woman with the scarf and the time I've spent on hold.

"What is it about the scarf?" says Ethan.

"What do you mean?"

"What does that have to do with anything?"

"Nothing. I liked it."

"Elizabeth is always fooling with her scarf."

"The scarf isn't the point. The point is the bowling alley."

"Well, I think that could be good for you. You need to get out more. It'll help you meet someone."

The crazy thing about Ethan is that even though he thinks marriage is tremendously difficult, he wants everyone he knows to wed as quickly as possible.

"I have a boyfriend. Lewis."

"Lewis, sure. So where's Lewis in all of this?"

"On a sit." I look at the gray felt of my cubicle wall.

"Maybe it'll help you meet someone who isn't always on a sit."

Lewis has been doing a lot of sits recently. When we met, he was a real-estate broker. He didn't know what a sit was. He'd just started going to a meditation group near his apartment to cope with stress. The group leader told him about long sits. "He says they'll help me overcome this plateau," Lewis said. After the first sit Lewis quit the firm, and since then he's been sitting for about a week every month. When he isn't on a sit he volunteers as a reader for a group that records books for the blind and dyslexic. He was going to answer their phones—most of the readers are actors—but when the head of the foundation heard Lewis speak she suggested he read. He has a good voice—low and scratchy. Lewis can afford to do all of this because his great-grandfather invented a heat resistant kind of plastic. His trust fund is so big that if he wants, he can sit for the rest of his life.

On my way home from work I stop at the bowling alley and look in. Everything is dark except for the lanes, which are lit up as though they're pathways to somewhere important. I try to remember the Laundromat: its chipped linoleum floor, big white machines, metal and plastic carts for moving wet clothes. But those are all features of my current Laundromat. Maybe I'm thinking of that.

Lewis calls in the evening, while I'm drafting an e-mail to the leader of a community group. The group is protesting a developer who plans to convert an old, disintegrating tenement nearby into condominiums. No one is living in the tenement; the bricks look rotten, the windows are boarded up, and the boards have started to fall apart. But it's overgrown with vines and is home to a lot of sparrows and a few nice-looking pigeons, which the community group is calling doves. They've started calling the whole building an ecosystem, and I heard they've written to the EPA for support. I tell them I'm writing with regard to the bowling alley that recently opened. I'm trying to figure out the next sentence when the phone rings.

"This fly got into the room," Lewis says. "The big kind."

"A black fly."

"It was floating around me for half an hour."

"That's a long time." Though is it? I don't know much about flies.

"Well, it felt like half an hour. Time does funny things when you're sitting."

"It stretches?"

"I can't describe it. Afterward, Elena said I'd done a great job. You know Elena? The leader of the sit."

"I thought you weren't supposed to talk. I thought you were supposed to let go of the idea of doing a good or bad job."

"We're not rigid. I have to go. I'm not supposed to be on the phone."

"Wait. Help me with this e-mail."

"Can't. Elena's coming. See you soon."

I've never met Elena, but Lewis has mentioned her before. I picture her with thin wrists and the earnest, confident demeanor of a person who lives her principles. I imagine her as someone I know, a woman whose family owns a few Italian restaurants near my parents' house. I see Lewis and my old neighbor side by side on the floor of a dusty old schoolroom, a fly dancing around their heads.

On the street a man shouts, "Did you see it?" I hear the music and feel it too, a thrumming in the back of my head. I go to the window. A group is clustered in front of the bowling alley. I finish my e-mail to the community board leader. *Very loud, very bright, disruptive to the community.*

The deputy leader of the community board is wearing a green coat that looks waterproof, even though it's not raining. "Call me Pamela," she says. "Not Pam." Her pants are rolled up and she has on thick brown socks. I walk her to the bowling alley. The windows are covered with powdery streaks, as though they've been cleaned with the wrong solution. Inside the place looks barren—pale lanes, shadowy gullies, plastic booths, and small tables. In the raw morning light, it's all pretty depressing.

"The truth is," Pamela says, "there isn't much we can do about it."

She says that the group has had the most success when they begin their action before a site has been developed; once something's there, it's hard to get rid of.

"I have to confess," she says, "this doesn't seem bad. I like bowling."

"But this isn't just a bowling alley," I say. "It's a club too. They play music all night."

She's peering in. "In the back—is that the bar?"

"How about an ordinance—after ten they have to turn off the music and dim the lights?"

Pamela shrugs. "I'm sorry I can't help."

At work I call the sheep guy. "GE," I say to the answering machine. "This is your publisher checking in about your contract. We're eager to move forward." I always say this when I'm tracking down contracts, but in his case it's true. There's a wool convention coming up and we'd like to have the book ready in time. I'm receiving e-mails from people high up in the company. The contracts manager in England wrote yesterday that I was holding everything up.

In the afternoon, Ethan asks me how things are going with the bowling alley.

I tell him about Pamela. "And I'm still waiting to hear from the people who *own* the bowling alley."

"You spoke to someone there?"

"I wrote an e-mail and some guy—Sam—wrote back. But since then—nothing."

"They always pick friendly sounding names. When I was in touch with the company about my stove, when the burner wasn't working, they signed their e-mails Jenny."

"You think they have people assume names? What do you think their real names are?"

"You think they have *people* responding to these complaints? They don't have real names. They're computers."

The day Lewis returns from his sit I leave work early to clean my apartment. Lewis usually comes straight to my place from the Berkshires and I imagine when things are neat the transition is a little smoother. Lewis's sitting practice has made him happier than when he was in real estate, and it's been mostly positive for me too. When we first met he worked long hours; I only saw him on the weekends. Now I see him all the time when he's not meditating. Sometimes he comes over in the late afternoon and assembles dinner for us. He doesn't cook, but he buys nice things: Marcona almonds, dates, white anchovies. He spent some time in Spain in his early twenties.

"Hi," he says, coming through the door.

I kiss one of his cheeks and it's cold. He drops his bag in my entryway and lies on my couch.

"I've been thinking about your bowling problem."

"Can you hear it? The music?"

It's around nine and the music has just started. I hear it faintly in the back of my head.

"Music? No. But I think it's like that fly." He says the bowling alley could my teacher; I'm meant to learn something from it.

"What? What did you learn from the fly?"

"I can't describe it." He suggests we take up bowling, at least give it a try. He says that he discussed the whole thing with Elena on the car ride home.

"You rode back with her?"

"I gave her a lift."

On the street someone yells strike.

"Elena thinks the bowling alley opened to show you something about yourself. But there's no rush figuring it out. You may need to be with it for a while."

"Some of us have jobs," I say. "We can't just be with problems. Some of us don't have time to sit for three months a year." Though I spend all day at work sitting. And at home I sit a lot too, because by the time I get home I'm worn out. "What does Elena do anyway?"

"*Elena* is retired. She used to be a special-ed teacher for the city. She has a pension. What's your problem?"

The picture I have of Lewis and the brown-haired girl disappears. In its place I see Lewis and an older person, someone who looks like Pamela, the deputy leader of the community board. I see her thick socks. But that may not be right either. I remember a teacher I had, a graceful woman with short white hair who always wore heels.

"I don't understand this part of your life," I say. "It's a big mystery. I'm completely left out."

"Here." Lewis pulls the cushions off the couch and for the next half hour we sit on the floor and try to be with the bowling alley, and each other, and what he calls my well of pent-up aggression.

In the morning I have a message from a woman who sounds old. The connection is bad. "Please don't call," she says. "GE has passed away." She keeps talking, but I can't understand anything else.

I walk around the gray cubicle wall to Ethan's desk. He's eating a bagel; his fingers are shiny with butter. His face surprises me with how real it is, how thick and pink and white.

"I forgot about these." He lifts the bagel. "From the place next door?"

"GE died," I say.

"Who?"

"GE."

"Oh, the sheep." Ethan puts down the bagel. "That's a shame."

Back at my desk, I think about the wool conference, dozens of sheep farmers roaming the convention empty handed, no book to buy, no one to explain their history. I think about my messages to GE, how I used the word "eager." My problem is that I take things personally. Lewis and I decided this last night and it was a relief. Not everything has to do with me. Even the things that have something to do with me, like this contract, don't have *that much* to do with me.

I picture the woman—Elliot's sister? lover? wife?—listening to my messages in a quiet house. I've never seen GE, but there's an author photo on the book he published ten years ago. He looks like Charles Darwin, only with fewer wrinkles and a smaller beard.

I think about Elena, the pension check that comes to her each month from the government. It's probably an oversized green check, like the one I get for my tax rebate. I think about my old teacher, sitting at her desk barefoot, each of her shoes, her heels, in a different part of the room, as if she'd just walked out of them. I think about the man on the street yelling "strike" and Pamela bowling. I think about Ethan's oatmeal and my phone calls to the district councilman and borough president. I see them on the floors of their offices, buried in message slips.

In the afternoon I leave more messages for the councilman and president. I give my name and relate the content of my previous calls. "I want to withdraw my complaint," I say.

After work I go to the bowling alley to have a mojito. When I open my wallet, though, the green paper isn't there, and the person at the bar is a short, burly, blond man, not the bartender-manager I met, no two-for-one specials here. I'm sorry not to see the bald man whom now, in memory, I have a fondness for, but I order a drink anyway, happy to pay for it.

PESTS

Karen woke up because the puppy was whining.

"It's OK, Tas," she said. She put her finger in the crate, felt his cold, damp nose.

There was a clatter from the other room. She poked Jeremy.

"What?" he said. It was dark and she couldn't see his face, only bulky shadows, his shoulders and head.

It continued: crunching, like someone stepping on glass, a bang. Something might have fallen down; it had happened before. The portrait of Jeremy's grandfather, which they'd hung as a joke, but which was no longer a joke for Jeremy, had come loose from the wall. That was like a gunshot. This was quieter, like a picture falling in another apartment, although it also sounded close. It could have been a small thing—the photo of the barn, the woodcut she'd bought in New Mexico. Tas rattled the door of his crate and there was another bang. The jug of eucalyptus? Were they being robbed?

Jeremy rushed out of the room and Karen sat up, listening to his footsteps. Then he was back, his face in the doorway. She could see the suggestion of his nose, long and knobby.

"What is it?" she said.

"Wait." He left.

"What?" Karen called.

"Mice."

She drew the sheet up and felt a tickle along her hairline. But mice couldn't hurt you. "What fell?"

"The vase. It didn't break." There was a tap, tap, tap in the other room. "Hang on."

Tas was quiet and Karen fell asleep.

It was raining. The exterminator had left his jacket and shoes in the hall, and his socks made wet prints on the floor. Karen gave him a towel, and he ruffled it through his hair and used it to wipe his arms. Then he draped it over his head, like an athlete on the sidelines.

"Seven."

"Seven mice?" asked Karen.

"Your husband said five to seven."

Jeremy had left early. He'd emailed to say he'd called the exterminator, and then this man, Eli, had rung the buzzer.

"Jumping," said Eli.

"Do they do that?" asked Karen. "It was late and Jeremy's—exhausted."

Eli looked away. He didn't want to hear about Jeremy's work and tiredness. But Karen hated thinking about infestations. Her friend Charlotte recently had termites. She'd written a note asking them to leave, after reading about the method in a magazine. Karen could imagine the sort of magazine that dispensed this advice, the kind sold in health food stores with seasonal vegetables on the cover.

Hello termites, Charlotte wrote.

"What are the chances termites call themselves termites," Karen said to Jeremy.

"Good point," said Jeremy.

"Also—"

Jeremy said, "No need. You made your case."

Eli was picking at a hangnail. He'd left a long break in their conversation.

"Do mice really jump?" Karen asked again.

"Sometimes they do." He said it could have been a territorial dispute. Every building had a nest of rodents, usually in the basement. He said, "When the mother nest is disturbed, the animals are flushed out. They fight for ground."

There had been a man in the basement tinkering with the boiler for a few days. Fiona on two was in charge of it. The nest would be in the corner, in a coil of tubing that belonged to Paul on three. Karen imagined the stirring in the center of the coil as the animals made room. She shifted, trying to nudge the image out of her head.

"You're lucky it's mice," Eli said. "Some buildings have rats."

Tas, who'd been lying at Karen's feet, a little pile of hay, looked up. There was a dog he played with at the park named Rat.

"It's OK, Tas." Karen scratched his neck.

Eli turned away again, lowered his eyelids. Karen saw that his boundaries were very firm. His gaze stopped at the counter where there were a couple of unwashed mugs and a sliced apple going brown. Karen could guess his thoughts—that she deserved her mice or rats or whatever.

"I read that rats are aggressive," Karen said, trying to decide if, in the dark, Jeremy could tell the difference between a mouse and a rat.

"Sure," Eli said. "They'll attack."

"But mice can't hurt you."

"They carry disease. Rats do too."

Tas began to whine.

"Hey, hey, hey," Karen said.

Eli stood up. "I can't do it now—I have an appointment. You'll be around this afternoon?"

"I should be." Karen didn't like people to think she was too free. "I can be."

When she was confident she wouldn't run into Eli on the street, she took Tas out. It was raining hard—harder than had been suggested by the radio or Eli's hair and socks. On the radio, the man had said, "Rain today, heavy at times," casually, but this weather was an event. Karen was in her boots and jacket and had an umbrella, but she was still getting wet.

"Come on, Tassie." She dragged him to a tree. "Potty."

Tas sniffed. He was distracted by the rain and didn't want to touch the wet leaves in his usual place. They were mulchy and foamy.

"Let's go." Karen pulled him along forcefully and then, noticing a woman at the end of the street, more gently. "Tassie Tas." She lured him with a piece of lamb lung. There was a relatively dry spot under a big tree where the ground looked cultivated— rows of green bundles. Ordinarily, Karen would not have encouraged Tas to pee on somebody's garden, but the morning wasn't ordinary. Cars were using their headlights. There was a flicker of lightning.

"OK," she said. "Potty."

Tas squatted and released a thin stream, half onto a plant, half onto his back leg.

"Good dog," she said. "What a good boy."

At home, she put on the radio and walked slowly around her apartment, searching for signs of mice. She had the tickling feeling on her neck. A mouse might jump out from anywhere. She imagined one scuttling across her foot, as had a large beetle at the office where she used to work.

Eli called to say that he would come tomorrow, not today.

"That's completely fine," Karen said, though he hadn't asked whether it was fine. "You mentioned illness?" she said. "Anything I should worry about?"

"It's good to get rid of them," he said.

"Oh, I wasn't—I was just curious."

"We'll get it taken care of."

Left without a plan for the afternoon, Karen picked up a book, put it down, opened another, put it down. She went through book after book, including a few she'd been working on for years—a novel based on the Kennedys, an investigation of a big seed company, *Moby-Dick*. In the end, she watched a few hours of a television show about real-estate brokers in Atlanta.

At seven, Jeremy called to say he'd be another couple of hours at work. Karen took her time making dinner—noodles with broccoli—and when he arrived she was melting an anchovy in oil. He bent down to kiss Tas and then jumped up.

"There!" he said.

Karen looked where he was pointing, but she didn't see anything. She'd left books on the table, a kind of evidence about her afternoon, but Jeremy wouldn't know that.

"If it's a cockroach," she said, "I don't want to see it. Just throw it out."

"A mouse," said Jeremy. "It was a mouse." He walked to the edge of the room, where there was a gap between the floor and the baseboard. "That's where it went."

"A mouse couldn't fit through that," Karen said.

"Mice are agile," said Jeremy. "They have little bones."

Karen thought of the tiny, melting anchovy bones. "It must have been a baby mouse."

"What did the guy say?"

"He's going to put some stuff down. He's coming back tomorrow."

Jeremy reached for a piece of broccoli.

"Stop it," Karen said. "Wait."

"OK." He backed away from her to the table.

Over dinner Jeremy said, "How's the job search?"

"Fine," said Karen. "But with Tas—I'm not sure it's the best time. I may look for more tutoring."

"Sure," said Jeremy. "I don't care."

Karen had recently quit her job at a conservation organization. Jeremy managed construction projects for a bank. He made a little more money every year.

"How's *your* work?" Karen said.

"Remember that guy Frank? The jerk?"

"The singer?" One of Jeremy's colleagues was in some kind of big-deal choir.

"Yeah, him. They fired him."

"That's horrible." It was shocking when someone was actually fired. At Karen's old job, there'd been a man who'd spend hours every day looking at Internet porn—and his computer faced out. Once in a while he was called into human resources to receive an official warning. As far as Karen knew, he was still employed.

"He tried to steal a scanner," Jeremy said. "He put it on a mail cart and got it into the elevator."

"Nobody saw him?"

"It was late. The security guard stopped him in the lobby. Now he's having tests."

"What tests?"

"X-rays? Something for his head."

"They fired him for that?"

"Joseph said he doesn't work for us anymore. That's all I know."

Tas woke up again in the night. The noises from the other room were different—padded sounds, like a bird trapped in a curtain. Jeremy wasn't in bed.

"Where are you?" Karen called.

He came in and reported that a gray mouse and a white mouse were wrestling, and a smaller white mouse was watching from the corner. "Like a human fight," he said. "Come—you have to see it."

"I don't want to. Get rid of them."

He left and Karen heard his voice—"That's it, that's it"—soft and coaxing, urging them back into the gap in the floor.

In the morning Eli called to say that he could not make it. Someone he knew was in the hospital.

"I'm so sorry," Karen said. "I hope everything is OK."

He said he would come tomorrow "rain or shine."

Karen browsed an employment website and saw a listing for an art history teacher in Atlanta—where the televised real-estate brokers lived. She imagined the early spring: warm and cool at once, dewy grass, red and blue flowers. She should have majored in art history, at least taken a class or two. There were no postings for the tristate area. She inspected Jeremy's mouse hole, which was not even a hole, just a bit of dark space. How *could* a mouse, even a baby, fit through that? She put a cookbook over it and decided to go out, to a coffee place she liked. There were always flowers in the window—right now, a narrow wooden branch with pink blossoms, a part of a cherry tree, Jeremy said.

She put peanut butter into a plastic toy for Tas. You were supposed to do and say the same thing every time you left a dog so that it all became routine. It lessened the stress of departure. Tas jumped against her in impatience.

"Off," she said. "Sit."

He lay down.

People should be left with treats, she thought, but you'd have to find something better than peanut butter—a TV series with unlimited episodes, or the kind of layer cake you only get at children's birthday parties and some weddings, or a Percocet. Paul on three had given her half a Percocet when she pulled a muscle in her neck. The two hours after she took it were the most carefree of her life.

If Jeremy could leave her with a Percocet, she'd be fine, but this was a housewife cliché. Maybe he could leave her with Charlotte. Charlotte and Brendan owned a restaurant in upstate New York and Karen and Jeremy had spent a couple of weeks with them last summer. Charlotte pointed out the different lettuces in her garden and taught Jeremy a way to chop an onion where you left the stem intact.

"This appeals to my sense of precision," Jeremy said, admiring the heap of white chips on the cutting board.

"What sense of precision?" Karen said.

One or two friends stopped by most days for lunch, or a walk, or a drink. Curled under the quilt in the guest bedroom, Jeremy said he wanted to move to the country.

"It's healthier," he said. "Everything about it."

Which was Karen's argument, with which he usually disagreed. She rolled onto her back. "You'd never leave the city."

"I would. Wait and see."

Tas's eyes tracked Karen's smallest movements while she spread the peanut butter. She tried to get it into all the little corners of the toy. "See you soon," she said, placing it on the floor.

Outside, the rain had paused but the air was wet. Just before she reached the café, there was a burst of thunder.

"How's it going?" The barista smiled at her. He was her favorite server, about her age with silky brown hair.

"I have mice!" Karen said.

"Mice?" He turned to pour her a cup of coffee. "My roommate had mice once. He said—this is gross."

"It's OK. I'm in this world." She thought about Charlotte's termites.

"He said the best way to get rid of them is to boil them."

Karen saw Jeremy dropping a mouse into her yellow soup pot. She saw its tail, stiffly curved, like a cane. "Boil them in what?"

"Water? It stops them from coming back—sends a warning to the others."

"Yeah?" She leaned against the counter.

"They sense something. Or the smell."

"I'll ask the exterminator about it."

"Let me know what happens."

She wandered over to the milk and sugar counter with a friendly feeling. She didn't know the barista's name, but she thought of him as Ben. She went to high school with two Bens, and he looked like someone she'd gone to high school with, although not like either of them. Maybe she'd met him at a party sometime during high school. Maybe they'd made out. More than that, she'd remember.

He came to the milk counter to swap out some of the pitchers. In profile he looked a little like Greg, Charlotte's boyfriend from a while ago, before she met Brendan.

"Sorry." Karen moved her cup out of the way.

Karen had never cheated on Jeremy, but he'd once cheated on her. It was soon after they met. He was on a business trip and a woman at a party showed him her stomach. He told it to her like a funny story, not a confession.

"What do you mean showed you her stomach?"

"Her belly button ring."

Karen tried to picture this. "What did you do?"

"I just stood there. That kind of thing hasn't happened to me since college."

"In college people were always lifting up their shirts for you?"

"That *kind* of thing."

"Then what did she do?"

"She kissed me." Jeremy sounded surprised, though surprised that it had happened or surprised that he was telling her, Karen wasn't sure.

"And then what?" She felt discomposed, like her hair was lifting and spreading around her head, but when she looked at a mirror she saw that it was together in a clump.

"Nothing much." Jeremy laughed.

Karen started to cry, very lightly.

"Don't do that," said Jeremy. He put his hand on her shoulder. "It wasn't anything. I wasn't sure about what this was." He pointed to her and then himself. "But that—it was so little." He ran his hand down her back. "Hey, hey," he said, in just the voice she now used with Tas.

"Could I have a glass of water?"

Jeremy brought a mug with elephants on it, the handle shaped like an elephant trunk.

"I don't know why I told you like that," he said. "What's the matter with me?"

"Your water tastes like chlorine."

"That's true everywhere in America. Except for your place. I noticed the first time I stayed over."

It was the only incident of its kind. They talked about it for a week and then they stopped talking about it. Once in a while Jeremy would bring it up.

"When am I going to live that down?" he'd say, out of nowhere.

Eventually, he moved into her place. Then the guy who owned the apartment, who'd moved to Vancouver, wanted to sell. Jeremy bought it for a good price—for almost no money, everyone said, though it was more money than Karen or most of Karen's friends had. But it wasn't much for New York real estate and Jeremy had cash on hand from a deceased, childless uncle. "I'm very liquid at the moment," he said. The good tasting water, the view of the Hudson and the downtown rooftops—all of it was theirs. And now the mice were theirs too, stowaway pets.

Karen spilled out some of her coffee to make room for milk, and a woman in a white jacket with wet, bare legs flapped into the café. It was the other barista and she was hunched over, her shoulders curled, as though her back were a shield.

At the counter she dropped her umbrella. "My friend from high school died last night," she said.

"Agatha!" Karen's coffee guy said. He lifted a section of the counter and she walked through. He hugged her.

The other customers scattered. An older woman in exercise clothes scooted to the door, and a man hustled his child to the table farthest from the counter. Karen pressed a lid onto her drink. It was callous to flee immediately, but listening was also wrong, and she couldn't pretend not to hear the conversation. The thing would be to disappear.

Agatha was weeping into the guy's chest.

"When did you find out?" He held her up and away from him.

"Just now," Agatha said. "Half an hour ago."

"The parents called you?"

"My other friend." She made it sound insubstantial. Her face was pale and shining. She was usually a bit scruffy—broken fingernails, eye makeup drifting to her cheeks—but today she looked fresh, washed by the rain. Her jacket sparkled.

REMEMBER HOW I TOLD YOU I LOVED YOU?

"Agatha," the guy said again. "Why are you here?" He was trying to sound sympathetic, but Karen heard the criticism. He wanted Agatha to take her pain away. Of course, Agatha probably should
leave. It was awful to think of her taking coffee orders.

Karen's barista pulled Agatha close again. He began whispering
to her and Karen slipped out. At home, she called Jeremy.

"I went to the coffee place and that guy was there. The nice one."

"I can't stand that guy."

"Then the other one came in."

"The girl? I like *her*. She's so angsty."

"Her friend died."

There was a honk on Jeremy's end.

"I didn't hear you," he said.

Karen sat down next to Tas on the sofa. She leaned her head
against the cushion. "Her friend just died. She was really upset."

"Yikes." Jeremy's voice was thin.

"I wonder *how* the friend died," said Karen. "She must have
been young." She pulled Tas onto her lap and smelled his head, felt
his heart beat against his ribs. He sighed irritably and moved away
from her without opening his eyes.

"Maybe a car accident," Jeremy said. "Some drunk driving thing.
Hey!"

There was a whooshing sound. Karen said, "Are you OK?"

"This woman shoved me with her umbrella."

"I'm sure not on purpose."

"She's using it as a plow. Did the mouse guy come?"

"Someone's in the hospital. He's coming tomorrow."

"It's like everyone's sick. I heard Frank has a brain tumor."

Karen had a sudden feeling of closeness to Jeremy, like bump-
ing into a good friend at the grocery store. It *was* like everyone was
sick. "That's frightening," she said.

"It's benign. I can't think about it. I'm getting all wet out here. Can I call you later?"

In the afternoon, the dog trainer, Anna, arrived to work on leave-it and drop-it and review what they'd learned about biting. She left a yellow slicker and a pair of pink boots in the hall. Her clothes were dry.

"Tell me about the bites," she said.

"He's playing," Karen said.

"Sure," said Anna. "But it stops being play when he nips some kid on the street and the parents sue you."

"I know."

"Or worse."

"I know." Karen had heard stories about dogs being destroyed for all sorts of crazy things: barking, chewing up some furniture, baring teeth—threats only, no action—at a neighbor. "That's why I want to make sure we're taking care of it."

Anna said, "But then, he's still a puppy."

"Yes."

"A baby."

Karen nodded.

"You have to let him be a puppy." Anna tilted her head, skeptical.

"Well, of course we don't want to repress him. That's the challenge."

"Not for him!" Anna bent down and scratched Tas's side. He sat on her feet, his ultimate gesture of approval.

This was how things went with Anna. Karen tried to mirror what she said, but Anna was always modifying, amending—sometimes she changed tacks completely—so they'd end up squared off. Tas did something similar at the dog park when Karen went to put on his leash. He evaded her.

Anna was Scandinavian—Norwegian or Swedish—and had al-most white hair. She'd lived in the US for decades, but Jeremy said she looked as though she'd come directly from a fjord. "Her clothes are always clean," he said. "She spends all day with dogs and she's always clean."

"Leave it," Anna said to Tas.

Tas looked away from the strip of rawhide.

"Good!" She gave him a treat.

"Now you." Anna gave Karen the rawhide.

Karen held it out to Tas, who licked the end of it.

"Leave it," Karen said.

"Make it sound fun," said Anna.

"Leave it," Karen said in a higher voice.

"You still sound just a tiny bit"—Anna smiled and paused, then spoke softly, like she and Karen were sharing a confidence—"angry," she said.

"Leave it." Karen was almost shouting. Tas continued to chew.

"Terrible," said Anna to Tas. She took away the rawhide.

"Terrible," Karen repeated.

"*You're* terrible," Anna said to Karen, pretending to be Tas.

"Next week?" Karen said, as Anna dipped a leg into a boot.

"Will Jeremy be around?" Anna asked.

"I don't know. Should he be?"

"It's better when everyone is here. Consistency. But you can just pass everything along."

She said it as though she knew that Karen could not pass any of it along. This was true—Jeremy did not listen to Karen's instructions. But Anna's tone also implied that Karen didn't know this, or that she didn't know that Anna thought this. But I do know, Karen wanted to say, phrased in a way that would make her sound powerful.

"I'll tell him to come," she said. "He'll be here."

"It doesn't matter." Anna was at the stairs.

"Oh, Anna? We have this mouse problem?"

She turned. "You have?"

"Jeremy saw mice," Karen said. "The exterminator mentioned diseases. Is there anything I should worry about with Tas?"

"If the guy you have puts down poison, you'll want to keep him away from that."

"Your presence was requested next week," Karen said to Jeremy that night. He'd brought home fish and chips from the place on the corner. The oily takeout bag was between them and a fried smell hung around the table. You couldn't hear the rain, but you could see it, a crosshatch outside the window. Karen moved the bag.

"You have to be here next week," she said again. "Monday night."

"Special occasion?"

"Dog training. Anna asked for you."

"She did, did she?"

"She did." Karen looked at Jeremy for a moment, adopting Eli's conversation strategy: silence.

Jeremy put four french fries into his mouth.

"Well," Karen said. "Why does she want you here so much?" Something was urging her to continue, a not-unpleasant pull in her stomach.

"I can't tell if you're serious."

Karen shrugged. Tas was watching her.

"Anna has a boyfriend," Jeremy said. "Remember? Willy or whatever his name is?"

Anna did have a boyfriend, whom she'd mentioned a few times in their early sessions. Wiley.

"She hasn't talked about him recently. Maybe they split up."

"And?" said Jeremy.

"And still. Why does she want you there?"

He seemed to mull this over. "Because she likes me."

"That's what I think. You think so too? She likes you?"

"I know she likes me."

"But why?"

Jeremy looked at her.

"You know what I mean."

"We understand each other," Jeremy said. "I think we had similar childhoods."

Karen assumed he meant that they both grew up with dogs. "And you like her."

"Yeah, I do like her."

"I don't like her at all."

He smiled. "Right."

"What?" Karen said.

"I *know* you don't like her."

"What do you mean—you *know*."

"Well, it's obvious."

"Would you like her if you were me?"

"If I were you?" said Jeremy. "No."

"But *you* like her."

"Jesus—" He stopped. "Do you want to get a new dog trainer?"

"Maybe. I know you don't."

"I don't care."

But they only needed a couple more sessions, and Karen no longer felt much interest in Anna, just a sharp irritation with Jeremy. "OK, we won't switch." She gathered the silverware. "Anyway, if you come next time, she'll show you how to do stay correctly."

Karen and Tas slept through the night and in the morning Jeremy claimed to have seen the mice again.

"I can't believe they didn't wake you. They were making a racket."

"How many this time?" Karen was rubbing lotion into her heels, trying to keep her feet away from Tas, who liked to lick it off.

"Five? Six?"

"Really."

Jeremy turned from his closet. "You think I'm making this up."

Karen pulled on a silk sock, a gift from somebody in Jeremy's family. "The exterminator's coming today."

The rain had stopped but it was gray. Karen had pain in her knee. The weather's getting into me, she thought. She returned to her books, including two that had arrived in the mail. This time she made headway. Ishmael boarded the Pequod. In one of the new ones, a man drank too much and fought with his girlfriend.

Eli arrived close to noon. Tas was excited, recognizing that he was a repeat visitor. Jeremy liked to talk about Tas's innate courtesy.

"You should write some sort of a manners book combined with a dog book," he said. "Wouldn't that be good? Or make it a blog."

"You should write that book," said Karen.

"I could, if I had time."

The plan was for Eli to put a poison powder and then steel wool into all of the holes in the apartment. Steel wool on top, to maximize the distance between Tas and the poison.

"Although he shouldn't be interested in it," said Eli.

"The trainer said to be careful," Karen said.

"Dogs aren't stupid."

Karen was on board, except that she only knew of one hole—the space Jeremy had shown her. Eli pointed to a place in the entryway where the floorboards stopped short of the wall. He said he expected there to be quite a few holes. "In old apartments, there usually are," he said. He was one of those people who preferred new construction. Jeremy's parents were the same way.

Eli walked along the edge of the apartment like Karen had the other day. He was more purposeful, though, and didn't seem nervous. He was like an animal stalking something, which was exactly what he was. Ever since they'd gotten Tas, Karen and Jeremy were struck by the ways in which people were truly animals. Jeremy said this had changed how he related to his colleagues. "Before I might be annoyed by someone asking questions all the time," Jeremy said. "Now I see it's insecurity or boredom or something. Matty is like the dog Artemis. The growly one? Not well socialized. But it's not his fault anymore than it's Tas's fault when he does the running thing."

"Zoomies," Karen said.

"Yeah," said Jeremy. "What?"

"On the Internet they call the running thing the zoomies."

Anna, on the other hand, stressed that dogs were like humans.

"Some people are kind of mean," she'd said. "Some people are pushy. Some are gentle. Some shy. Dogs can be the same. They let you know."

"How?" Karen said, wondering if Anna thought Tas was mean.

"My dog, for example," said Anna. "He's always been crotchety. Even as a puppy. But you can get him to do anything for food."

Eli patted handfuls of steel wool into the holes—he'd found five. "I'm surprised there aren't more," he said. Karen had a feeling that he was not rooting for her—that in a general way he was against her. As if sensing this, Tas clamped onto the hem of his pants and pulled.

"Drop it!" Karen said. Tas let go of the fabric and looked at Karen's legs. "Good," she said, and to Eli, "Sorry."

"These are old," Eli said, touching his trousers.

Karen peered at the gap he was working on. "Do you think they're coming through all these places?"

"There's no evidence of them. That doesn't mean they aren't coming or that they won't come."

No evidence. So Jeremy might be hallucinating the mice. But as long as the underlying cause wasn't too serious—just sleep deprivation, for example—an episode like this could bring them closer together. Karen would be supportive. If he had to quit his job, she'd figure out a way to make money. Maybe she'd work at the coffee place. Her eyes drifted to the books on the table. What would Jeremy do if he had to stop working for a while? Move to the country and write the dog manners blog. Anna would read it. Or piano. At some point before they met, she knew, he'd taken a few lessons.

Eli shouted. It must have been Eli, though the sound was loud and startling, and he until now had been so contained. But Eli was the only other person in the apartment and he was holding his ankle.

So there were mice—and they attacked?

"What happened? Are you OK?"

"Your dog." Tas was lying next to Eli, resting his head on his paws, which were stretched out in front of him.

"He bit you?"

Eli sat on the couch now, pulling down his sock. There was a little purple bruise in the hollow beneath his ankle. In the center of the bruise was a darker spot where the skin had punctured—just barely. Eli's face was clenched.

"Let me get you some water," Karen said. "Tas." She herded him out of the room. "You're terrible."

Eli refused the water. He wanted to leave. He said he was finished and had to get to the hospital.

"Oh," said Karen. "Your friend is still sick?"

"My brother."

"Your brother." She put her hand on her chest. "How is he?"

"Weak. It took them a while to figure it out what it was."

"But he'll be OK?"

Eli shrugged.

You weren't supposed to pry, ask for details. People told you what they wanted you to know. Karen waited and after a moment said, "I'm so sorry about your foot. It's our fault—we need to be more stern. He's a good dog."

"I have dogs," said Eli. Whether he meant this sympathetically, she couldn't tell.

She made chicken for dinner. She was using a new method, one where you didn't check on the meat. The pieces of chicken legs and chicken breast were in her big silver pan, underneath the lid, cooking unseen. Eli called to say that at the hospital *he'd* seen a doctor to have the wound checked. Wound? Karen thought. He said he'd be sending her the bill.

When she put down the phone, she began to weep a little. Tas looked at her critically. She stopped crying and called Charlotte.

"My dog bit the exterminator," she said. "Jeremy's seeing mice. I don't know if they're real. He's working so much, you know?"

"My cat died this morning," Charlotte said. "The one with the leg."

One of Charlotte's kittens was born with a misshapen leg and she carried it with her in a sling. She'd e-mailed Karen a picture and Karen had sent her a blue and yellow shawl to use a couple of months ago.

"Oh," said Karen. "I'm sorry."

Charlotte sighed. "We buried her near the porch." But then her voice changed. "It was a beautiful service."

Karen laughed. "Did Brendan speak?"

"Too emotional. You know how he gets. But it's the first time he's worn a tie since the wedding."

There was a voice in the background.

"OK OK," said Charlotte. "He says hi. I've gotta run."

Karen plated the chicken and put the plates on the microwave, where Tas couldn't reach them, until Jeremy got home. Everyone *was* sick. Or worse. Charlotte was Karen's closest friend—she made Karen feel like herself—but Eli, who refused to really talk to her, had been a bigger part of her life this week. They'd been in constant touch. Now she'd never see him again, unless he decided to sue her. She put her hand on Tas's head. If needed, she'd protect him.

When Jeremy got home she told him about the bite.

"You did what?" Jeremy said to Tas.

"It was awful," said Karen. "They put Eli on antibiotics for the wound. Precautionary."

"But was there a wound?"

"Well," said Karen happily. " *That's* the thing."

ACKNOWLEDGMENTS

I'm grateful to my teachers, my friends, and my family, for their insight and help at every stage of writing and revising these stories.

Particular thanks to Ed Park, Binnie Kirshenbaum, Carmen Johnson, David McCormick, Bridget McCarthy, Stefanie Victor, Sarah Donato, Sonny von Gutfeld, Sophie Pinkham, Eugene Linden, Mary Rasenberger, Madelaine Gill, and, especially, David Feinberg, for his generous and invaluable reading and editing. And thanks to Forth, for all and for everything.

ABOUT THE AUTHOR

Gillian Linden received her MFA from Columbia University. She is a 2011 winner of the Henfield Prize in fiction. She lives in Brooklyn with her husband.

Made in United States
Troutdale, OR
04/25/2024

19447002R00076